TWO
REBELS FROM THE
ALTAMAHA

William A. Bowers Jr.

ISBN: 978-0-5786126-3-8
Library of Congress Control Number: 2019918816
Published by

Swampfox Publishing Company

Edited by Deloris W. Bowers, Elizabeth B. Hall, and Cherry W. Platt
Cover and Interior Design by William A. Bowers, III
Cover and Interior Art by Donna Dunwoody

Printed in USA for Swampfox Publishing Company

TABLE OF CONTENTS

Chapter One: Jinin' Up   1

Chapter Two: Into Battle   15

Chapter Three: South Mountain
    and the Bloodiest Day   29

Chapter Four: To the Carolinas   49

Chapter Five: Olustee   64

Chapter Six: Back to Virginia   73

Chapter Seven: North Carolina Again   85

Chapter Eight: The Last Battle   91

Chapter Nine: Going Home   101

Chapter Ten: Courtin'   107

A

ILLUSTRATIONS
By Donna Dunwoody

Cover	"Two Rebels in action"
Campfire	1
Campsite	15
General Lee	29
Two in Battle	49
Arkansas Toothpick	64
Stitching up the Leg	73
Wooden Canteen	85
Yankee Canteen	91
Soldiers Companion	101
Sally and Mary	107
Willie and Randall at the Whirl Hole	113
First Cabin	114

PREFACE

When we were young my cousin, Randall, and I would draw Confederates whippin' Yankees on the margins of paper we would retrieve from the 2nd grade wastebasket. (I think paper was rationed then in our school) In the eighth grade, we took a class trip to Atlanta and visited Stone Mountain and the Cyclorama. We were both inspired although he took his to the point of drawing a mural with crayons on freezer paper. It depicted the Cyclorama and circumnavigated our eighth grade history room.

My great grandmother was sister to his great grandfather. They both lived in the section of Appling County, Georgia where the characters in this book originated.

This is a historic novel. All the Characters in this story were imaginary all the events they were involved in were actual. The 27th Georgia Infantry was in forty-four engagements in Florida, South Carolina, North Carolina, Virginia and Maryland. The Company from Appling County, which was a part of the 27th Georgia, suffered a one hundred twenty-five percent casualty rate, with one of my cousins being wounded four times. He was still fighting at Bentonville, North Carolina (the last battle of the war in the East).

These Confederate soldiers came home to try to rebuild what had remained, for the most part, untended and in a disheveled state.

I dedicate this work to my lifelong friend, E Randall Floyd. He and I became interested in this era when we were about seven years old. And the fire still burns to this day.

Chapter One: Jinin' Up

It was still cold in South Georgia when the hot news began racing around Appling County that Georgia had seceded from the Union. Although work went on, any time two young men got close together, they would talk of war. It was no different out on the Altamaha River, where although the crops were being tended, the young men's minds were constantly thinking of war. Word had come out that the Appling Volunteers, one of the militia units from Appling County, were beginning to form up and train near the little church called Bethel. Willie could hardly wait. The excitement of joining the military consumed him. He and his friend Randall could talk of nothing else. Although they were only fifteen, they were totally consumed with the fire of secession. They lived on adjoining farms so they saw one another frequently. They would meet up at Ten Mile Creek and discuss the upcoming war while trying to catch an "old butter cat" on a line.

Sunday at church, all the young boys gathered at the big oak tree near the front of the church and began to talk of "jinin' up". Their excitement rose when they heard that the men were going to drill that afternoon in the field by the church. When this started, they left the little children behind and went to the edge of the field to see what drilling really meant. The beginning of the drilling consisted of each man cutting about a five foot long sapling and stripping all the limbs from it. Since they had no rifles, the saplings would have to do for the time being. The men who were giving them instruction were veterans of the Indian Wars and even some soldiers from the War of 1812. They instructed the men on how to "close order drill" and began to call out commands like "by files right", "shoulder arms" and "forward march". The boys were amazed at how quickly their fathers and uncles and neighbors caught on. They desired so much to be out there and join them but they were too young to be considered a man. They had to be content to watch for now.

The men in that militia company eventually were sent to defend Savannah and the Georgia coast and ports. Willie's father was one of those men, although he was almost forty five years old. Willie wanted to go also, but his mother would not allow it. He would muse all day of going to war and being a man. Sometimes it would interfere with his work around the farm. He would be scolded for his inaction at his duties. With his father gone to war, more of the manly chores became his.

In the summer of 1861, he and Randall turned sixteen and wanted to serve the Confederacy as soldiers. The recruiting officer for the Appling Grays, a company that had left in August to go to Camp Stephens in Griffin, Georgia, was recruiting in Holmesville. This company was a part of the Twenty-seventh Georgia Regiment. He and Randall discussed the future, and the two of them caught a ride on a wagon headed for Holmesville. They had never been to Holmesville. It was the county seat of Appling County and where most of the commerce went on. This is where the small courthouse had been built there for trials and where the county records were located. They could not imagine that there were ten business activities going on there. John Graham had a store, and John Comas (a real honest to goodness Spaniard) had one too. The only store near where they lived was Middleton's store, in close proximity to where Stafford's Ferry crossed the mighty Altamaha River. This was a new world to them. They found the recruiter and both signed up with the

2

Appling Grays. The Recruiter told them that the wagon with recruits would be leaving in a couple of days to head north to Griffin, Georgia.

The trip had taken the better part of the day to get there. Now he and Randall were in Holmesville with two days to spend and nothing in particular to do. They looked around and everyone seemed so busy. Shopkeepers, the operator of the grits mill and just the people in general were bustling with activity. There was a bustle around the courthouse too, because there was a trial going on. Someone said there were more people in town than normal because of the trial. They edged close to the courthouse to see what was going on. They heard some of the people discussing the merits of the trial. It seemed that someone was accused of hog stealing. There was something about the mark on the ear that had been changed, but the owner of the hog still knew that it was his. In that day and time, hog stealing was a serious offense. They decided that the trial was not nearly as interesting to them as it was to the rest of the folks, so they moved on down the little clay street. Then they walked by the schoolhouse and could see the children inside. It was not too very long ago that they were in school. Now they were too old.

They had to quickly step out of the street because the freight wagon was coming through and the two horses hitched to the wagon did not look very friendly. They sat down in the shade of a large live oak tree to eat. Willie reached in his haversack pulling out a piece of cornbread that he had taken from his mother's pie safe. The cornbread and three pieces of fatback were all he had, and he knew he could eat them all at one sitting. He resolved to keep some in reserve for later. Randall also had something to eat because the boys had planned this carefully. When you get older, and become a man you need to act like one and think about what you're going to do ahead of time. After eating a little, they began to look for some shelter where they could spend the night. Willie had an old small quilt and Randall had an old blanket, both rolled up and tied with ropes so they could swing it over their shoulders.

The next two days were uneventful, but at the crack of day on the third morning, they were there with eight other young boys and the recruiter. They all piled in the back of the wagon that was provided at that location for them and prepared for the long trip. This was a much longer trip than they could imagine because Holmesville was as far as they had ever been from home in their life. The ten new recruits were embarking on an adventure of a lifetime. They settled in on the forage that was laid in the wagon to feed the horses. As they traveled through parts of the county never seen before, they were amazed. They traveled through an area that was called Hall, because the famous Seaborn Hall lived there. Seaborn was one of the two men sent by Appling County to Milledgeville to the secession convention in January of 1861. Everyone knew about Seaborn Hall. He was about as prominent as anyone in Appling County could get. He was a large landowner, he had been in the Georgia Legislature and Senate and he owned several large tracts of land in the county. Not long after passing Hall, they made their way to Towns Bluff Ferry, which was also owned by Seaborn Hall. They had been across Stafford's Ferry down where they lived to get on the Tattnall County side of the river and had heard there were other ferries across the mighty Altamaha. As the ferry operator began to make the passage across the river, they were excited, because now they were going to be in Montgomery County. Now they were going to see the great expanse of their state and see and do things that none of their friends had ever done.

They spent the night by a church called Charlotte and were delighted to find that the recruiter had provided bread and dried meat for them so they didn't have to go into their stash. They sat around the fire that night, not to warm because it was not cold, but just to bask in the glow of the firelight. Eventually, they all went to sleep in a circle around the fire. The next morning they were awakened early as the wagon was being hitched to the two horses. They started again on their travel. They continued to be amazed at all the new country and how the terrain began to change. It was hillier than it was where they lived. They passed through Mount Vernon, the county seat of Montgomery County and made their way toward Dublin. It took almost two days to make the trip to Dublin, due to the fact that they had to cross the Oconee River to get there. The Oconee is one of the two major rivers in Georgia that come together, not too far upstream from Towns Bluff, to form the Altamaha. Finally, after two more days, they made it to the state capital of Milledgeville. They had never seen a town of this size and they were just amazed at how many people and businesses located there. Then they saw the state capital, where the ordinance of secession was signed. They actually got to sleep under a roof that night, because they were put up in the barracks of

4

Georgia Military Institute located there. They were well fed and slept far more comfortably than they had slept on the ground for the last few days.

Willie and Randall had never seen a train before. The next day they boarded the train on the Central Railroad and Banking Company line at Milledgeville. This was entirely a new experience for them with the train's engine belching smoke and sparks that trailed behind it as it rolled down the tracks, at a faster rate than they'd ever been on a horse. They were off toward Macon, Georgia where they boarded the Macon to Atlanta line heading north. In one day's time, they covered more territory than they had in five days in the wagon. They also were joined by over two hundred young men as they piled into the box cars of the train for the journey. After less than a day's travel they piled out of the box car near Griffin, Georgia and walked in mass to Camp Stephens, which was the camp of instruction where the Appling Grays were encamped in training.

After reporting in to Captain Osgood A. Lee, they were fitted for uniforms and given brand-new pairs of brogan shoes to wear. They were also given other accouterments to finish out their uniform. A belt with a CSA buckle on it and a real wooden canteen were issued to them along with a haversack. The next day they began to train on close order drill. Willie had heard some of those orders before at Bethel, where the Appling Volunteers were training. They drilled all day long. His feet hurt from trying to break in the shoes that obviously didn't fit him, when one of the soldiers in the company told him to wet the shoes down and march in them until they dried and then they would fit. You'd also be able to tell which one was the left foot and the right foot because they would shape to his feet. Willie shared this with Randall. The next day they broke their shoes in. Their feet still hurt, but at the end of the day when the shoes dried, they could actually tell which one was which. Day after day they trained, drilled, marched up and down the parade field and generally learned about soldiering.

One afternoon as they were sitting on a log, in front of their tent Randall asked, "Willie, what do you think wars gonna be like?"

"I expect it's gonna be a lot of shootin' and killing and such," replied Willie.

"From the looks of what we doin' here, look like they gone be a lot a marchin' too," remarked Randall, "cause' we doing a lot of marchin' here at this place."

Willy retorted, "I shore am glad these old brogans are broke in. I thought they were gonna' kill my feet to begin with. That reminds me, I got to warsh these socks cause' they are getting a might ripe."

"Is that what I been 'a smellin'?" said Randall, chuckling as he held his nose between his thumb and first finger.

Willy mused, "I wonder when we gonna get muskets. It's gonna be hard to shoot at Yankees with our fingers. I hear that there's a shortage of muskets in Georgia right now. There is lots more soldiers than there is muskets right now."

"To be sure we'll get some before they send us to Richmond. I hear that's where we a'goin'," Randall stated.

"Here comes the Corporal, maybe he knows." Willie said, getting to his feet and stepping out in front of the Corporal in order to stop him. "Corporal, could you stop here a minute and talk to us?" The company had elected officers before they got there, and this was one of the corporals that were elected by the men.

The Corporal stopped and inquired, "What's on you boys' minds?"

"Corporal, we was a wonderin' when we gonna be issued muskets?" inquired Willie.

"Don't know for shore, but we better get them soon, because I heard the Lieutenant say that we would be heading out for Richmond pretty quick. I know they won't send us there without something to shoot at them Yankees with," answered the Corporal.

Late in October, the buzz around the camp was that they would be heading north to Virginia. There were eleven companies of South Georgia Militia that had initially gone to Camp Stephens. Ten of the companies were formed into the Twenty-sixth Georgia Volunteer Infantry. The other company, the Appling Grays was placed in the Twenty-seventh Georgia Volunteer Infantry along with companies from Middle Georgia, West Georgia and North Georgia. There were thousands of soldiers at Camp Stephens and much hustling and bustling around the company's encampment. Each company was camped together, and the tents, which they had been furnished, were in orderly rows. Randall had gotten sick shortly after they arrived, and it took him four or five days to get over what the men were calling "camp fever". Finally, he returned to his training. There were lots of men sick in the Regiment when they loaded on the train to head to Richmond, Virginia. Several had to be left behind, because they were too sick to travel. The train ride to Richmond was much longer than from Milledgeville to Griffin. Like the earlier ride they were in boxcars where they laid around, or sat around leaning up against the walls looking out the open doors at the change in scenery. Willie was totally amazed the first time he saw the mountains. Being from South Georgia, it was hard to imagine that land could go straight up so tall, so high in the sky. There were even clouds around the tops of the mountains. Somebody told him that's why they called them the Smoky Mountains.

When they arrived in Richmond, it was an unbelievable and awe-inspiring sight to see the capital of the Confederacy and just how big it was. Perched there on the James River atop towering bluffs was the center of commerce of the state of Virginia. They had never seen so many buildings in their lives. The city was all a bustle as they unloaded from the boxcars, formed up into their companies and took up a line of march toward the area in which they would encamp for the next few days, as they awaited orders. Several of the men had gotten sick on the trip and were placed in Richmond hospitals to recover. Willie heard the names of diseases that he had never heard before. He and Randall were both in good health so they were very hopeful that they wouldn't catch anything else.

The strangest thing about the Twenty-seventh Georgia arriving in Richmond, eager to go into the fight, was that when they arrived, they were still without any muskets. The state of Georgia still did not have enough guns to outfit all the troops. Although they had some muskets at Camp Stephens for them to learn how to carry, shoot and care for, they were not issued any to carry to Virginia. They had learned to "load by nine's", which was a nine step process to load a musket, at Griffin but had nothing to load and nothing to load into at that point.

Randall asked, "Willie, how we gonna fight when we ain't got nothing to shoot?"

Willie replied, "Why Randall, you know how to wrestle and fist fight don't you. I'm sure you can take one of them boards over there and whop a Yankee on the head with it."

"You trying to be funny, Willie? It don't sound too funny to me if them Yankees are shootin' real mini balls at us," Randall said.

Both boys got a good laugh out of that retort. Willie had always been a little on the funny side and could make Randall laugh easier than anybody else. They were tight and were the very best of friends. They had vowed to look after each other in this war. Each had sworn to make sure that both of them made it back home afterwards. That's what friends were for, wasn't it?

In a few days they "struck camp", and boarded another train headed toward Charlottesville, Virginia. Willie had read in school that Monticello, Thomas Jefferson's home, was in Charlottesville. They changed trains and headed to Camp Pickney near Manassas Junction, located close to the Virginia-Maryland border and really not far from Washington D. C., the federal capital.. On November 15, they arrived at Camp Pickney and were assigned an area for the Twenty-seventh Georgia to set up camp. The tents were all arranged in almost perfect rows grouped into companies and then even sub grouped farther into platoons.

Randall was Willie's mess mate, and they ate together daily. Meals usually would consist of some kind of bread, mostly cornbread and mostly some type of pork, salt pork or bacon. Sometimes they would have boiled beef. Willie and Randall were not used to beef, with the exception of the dried beef they used to dry and salt down, on the rare occasion when they killed a cow. Cows were mostly for milking, and only when a little bull would be born and they made him into a steer would he be fattened out for butchering. But they ate pretty well, although sometimes Willie would miss his mother's cooking. He had never realized how well she could prepare food for his taste. He had written several letters to her and worried about her a lot. One day he received a letter from her, and he could hardly wait to open it up. He opened it up and began to read. She at first scolded him for leaving and not telling her where he was going. And then she told him that his father was still somewhere over around Savannah, at a place called Red Bluff. She went on to tell that they hadn't seen much action around Savannah, but that the federal Navy was in the mouth of the Savannah River and had bombarded Fort Pulaski until the Confederates had to evacuate it and turn it over to them.

She also told what was going on around home and told him about his little sister Lizzie's activities. She was smart as a whip in school and had said she wanted to be a schoolteacher when she grew up. She told him of his friends who had also gone off to war, after he and Randall left. She sold one of the milk cows with a calf to get a little extra money to purchase staple goods. She also told him that Randall's mother was just sick because she hadn't heard from him and for him to help Randall write her a letter. It was great to hear from home, and it made him homesick a little bit, but he was a man now and had to put up with things like that.

They would drill and march every day, sharpening their soldiering skills for when they were needed. They still had no guns and had no idea how they would fight the enemy when the time came. But they pressed on. Willie had met Lieutenant Alfred Hall who was Seaborn Hall's son and Captain Lee's brother-in-law. Alfred was a jovial fellow and was dedicated to his duty as First Lieutenant of the Appling Grays. He had a pretty Colt's pistol on his side, which he had brought from Georgia, and he looked dapper in his uniform as he sometimes would lead them in their drills. Willie had even met some folks from some of the other companies in the Twenty-seventh. He had made friends with a Corporal from the Rutland Grays named John Wesley Bowers. They had struck up quite a friendship. John had left his family in lower Bibb County Georgia to come and fight. He was a slim fellow but possessed tremendous stamina. John's brother-in-law, James, was also in the Rutland Grays but was not nearly as personable as John was. He also had some friends from Marion and Schley Counties, who on their free time would come by and visit Willie and Randall. They would sit around and tell stories of home and how life was in their part of Georgia. These new friends kept camp life from becoming boring.

Willie came back to the tent one morning and reported to Randall that there was some activity going on and that the Twenty-seventh Georgia was going to build a bridge over the Occoquan River. He didn't know where the river was but he did know that they would be pulling out in the next day or so. Sure enough the next day's orders were given to "strike camp", which they did. They took up a line of march toward the northeast behind the convoy of wagons carrying materials. Upon arriving at the point where the bridge was to be built, they began to unload the materials. The river really didn't look very large to Willie and Randall, considering that the Altamaha was one of the largest rivers in the Eastern part of the United States. Somebody had said, "If two drops of water fall in Georgia, one will go down the Altamaha." That's a big river in anybody's book. The Altamaha supposedly ran into the Atlantic Ocean. Willy had learned in school that an ocean was a large body of water but he could not gather in his mind just how big it was. He hoped one day to get to see it. He had heard his father talking about taking a wagon with some tobacco and cotton that he had grown down to Darien, Georgia to trade for things that they needed and couldn't grow or make. He had seen the ocean because Darien was right there. The trip used to take a good long time because you first had to cross the Altamaha at Stafford's Ferry and then take the Darien to Hawkinsville stagecoach road in order to get there. Willy had wanted to make that trip with his father but the opportunity never came. One day he would see the ocean and maybe one day go to Darien.

They spent the rest of the day unloading the materials to be used to build the bridge. They said that it would be supervised by an engineer that had gone to West Point. Sure enough, the next day a dapper looking Colonel rode up on a black horse. He dismounted and took a large rolled up paper from his saddle bags. Colonel Smith, of the Twenty-seventh and some of the other officers gathered round him as he described what must be done and how they must do it. The men were broken up into details, Willie and Randall being some of the luckiest because their job was going to be in the water. Being old river rats they loved the water and both were excellent swimmers. For the next month, they worked on that bridge, although the water was cool, because it was winter. They didn't mind because there was always a roaring fire to get beside and warm, even if your teeth were chattering. It wouldn't take you long to warm up and dry out by a big fire. They also got a drink of some hot coffee. Randall really liked the taste of coffee but it was not something you could find every day. Sometimes the sutler would come by, but it would cost you an arm and leg just to get a little bag of it.

"What you reckon we gonna do when we finish this bridge?" Randall asked.

Willie replied, "I guess whatever them officers tell us to do. I hope they don't tell us to fight till we get some muskets. There may be another bridge somewhere that needs a buildin'."

Randall piped in and said, "When this is over, I might go to Milledgeville and go to that Georgia Military Academy where we slept that night. The food sure was good there and the beds were soft, lots softer than this old Virginia rocky ground."

They got word that privates Hester and Tuten had died in hospitals in Richmond. They were two that got sick on the way from Georgia. They also got word that privates Tomberlin and Jones had also died in hospitals. It didn't pay to get sick, because it looked like your chances of recovering were slim. They had left Private Crosby sick in Manassas and heard that he had died of pneumonia while they were working on the bridge. They also heard that a new recruitment officer had been sent back to Georgia to sign up more folks.

Willie had met one of his cousins, Benjamin Millikan, when he got to Griffin. In January, Ben was elected First Sergeant of the Appling Grays. Willie wondered if he would still have a good relationship with Ben now that he was the highest-ranking non-commissioned officer in the company. His worries were unfounded though, because Ben would stop on a regular basis to visit Willie and Randall and even had mess with them a few times.

In January 1862, they were issued Springfield Rifles, 58 caliber single shots.. Someone said these were rifles that were picked up in June, after the battle at Manassas, near where they were now stationed. These were rifles that the Yankee army had thrown down when they skedaddled trying to get back to the protection of Washington City. Old "Stonewall" Jackson had stood his ground and turned them Yankees around. They quickly got familiar with the new rifles. All of them learned to handle them and to clean them all over again. They took them out and fired them to see that they shot where they were supposed to. They were told that the Confederate armors had been checking out those rifles and were making sure they were fit for duty. They even said that some would have as many as seven charges and balls rammed in them, without ever having been fired. They had to dig all of those out to make them functional. They went out and practiced with them. "Loading by the nines", firing by rank, by file and all of the orders of firing that were taught them. Willie was a crack shot, and his rifle was true. He had shot his daddy's old squirrel rifle, a .36 caliber Kentucky rifle, at squirrels and raccoons and birds which he had hunted for table fare. Sergeant Ben even bragged on his shooting, which made him feel great to be noticed. Randall was an old swamper too. He was a good shot also. Sergeant Crosby said that they might be placed in his sharpshooters, out in the skirmish line when needed. It was all so exciting that they really could not take it all in. They quickly learned one thing about shooting those muskets. They had to keep them clean, because the saltpeter in the powder would rust and gum them up badly. You had to boil water on the fire and then pour it down the muzzle to flush the powder out of the barrel. You would keep pouring until the water ran clean out of the nipple. If the water was good and hot you could turn the rifle muzzle facing toward the ground and in just a minute the hot barrel would dry. Then all you had to do was to put a patch of cloth on your ramrod and put a little oil on it to protect the metal. Randall was so proud of his musket that every time he had a spare moment, Willie would see him over there wiping on it to make sure it was clean.

Now they were ready to shoot some Yankees. Randall wouldn't have to worry about wrestling and fist fighting. He could load up a mini ball and cap off the nipple and let loose. They were also given some cartridge pouches which would hold 60 paper cartridges which consist of a charge of powder and a lubricated mini ball. They were given a cap pouch and a handful of musket caps. They also were issued a frog, in which they carried their bayonet on their belt. The bayonet would fit over the sight of the musket. They were all decked out with accouterments and ready for war.

Chapter Two: Into Battle

       In early April the Twenty-seventh Georgia was assigned to
Featherstone's Brigade and was sent to Grover's Landing in Virginia.
Not long after that they were assigned to G. B. Anderson's Brigade.
While they were encamped, they heard that a fight had started near
Yorktown. The brigade was ordered there, and there was a buzz up and
down the lines as they headed to Grover's Landing. They moved to
Richmond and then on to Yorktown, where they were placed in the line.
On April 14th, they were sent forward in order to dislodge some union
sharpshooters who were harassing the Confederate artillerymen. Willie
and Randall were positioned behind an old fallen log and laid there while
awaiting orders. They looked off to the left and Sergeant Millikan was
headed their way, crouching low to avoid being shot. He got behind the
log with them and pointed to a clump of trees off in the distance.

The sergeant said, "You boys got a chance now to show what kind of shot you are. Off in that clump of trees are the union sharpshooters and they are wreaking havoc amongst our artillery pieces. Prime and cock weapons and if you see movement, shoot!"

"We'll do our best Sergeant," exclaimed Randall.

Willie piped up, "You can depend upon us Sergeant."

"I know we can," answered the Sergeant. "You two boys are two of the best shots in the company. That's why you're up here. Now take care of your business and make Appling County proud of you."

They lay there for a good while, and suddenly Willie noticed some movement in the right side of the clump of trees. Not on the ground, but up in the tree where he finally made out the green uniform of a federal sharpshooter. He drew a bead as fine as he had ever drawn on a squirrel or rabbit or a bird, and squeezed the trigger. He saw the green shape fall out of the tree and tumble to the ground. Just then Randall cut loose and another figure fell from a nearby tree. They both quickly reloaded another charge into their muskets and waited for more movement. They must've laid there for an hour or so when the Sergeant returned and told them to slip back and fall into line, as the rest of the Union sharpshooters had just been seen evacuating the little clump of trees. They moved back, joining with the ranks of the rest of the men as the Twenty-seventh began to pull out and head toward Williamsburg. They marched all the way to Williamsburg and then started marching on toward Richmond. They had made it about four or five miles out of town and were ordered to about face and to march back toward Williamsburg at the double quick. When the Regiment arrived back in Williamsburg, after traversing the terribly muddy roads with the wet and rainy and soggy conditions, they quickly threw off their blankets and haversacks and everything that could get in the way of a fight and piled them on the ground, rushing on into line. Willie and Randall were running at a full gallop with their muskets held in front of them. They went to the left of the town of Williamsburg and took up one position which they held for several hours. Then they were moved into a large wheat field. They remained there all night long. The boys were cold and tired and hungry, but they stayed right there in the place where they were assigned. They could hear the movement of the enemy at night, and about 1 o'clock in the morning, they were both called by the Sergeant for picket duty in front of the line. They really didn't mind it, because they were too cold and too hungry to sleep anyway. So they took their position out front to protect their company from a surprise attack. They would act as skirmishers and begin to fire at any enemy that would cross toward them, in order to give their company time to grab their muskets and prepare for action.

They didn't have to wait long, for at 2 o'clock they were ordered to pull back and form up with the company. They began the evacuation and again headed toward Richmond. They arrived at a long bridge and struck camp, cooked rations and began to warm by the fires.

Randall, while stoking the fire to heat up the coffee water remarked, "That was a bout a muddy, messy place we were in back there. Somebody said that Williamsburg was the second capital of Virginia after Jamestown. My granny said we had people at Jamestown, but I don't know why they wanted to live in that muddy place."

"You know a lot of the original settlers of Appling County in the 1820s came from families in the Carolinas, and they may have come from Virginia so your granny could be right. She might've been old enough to know. She looks like she's old as dirt anyway," replied Willie.

"Don't you talk about my granny that way," answered Randall. "She ain't no older than that granny of yours."

"I was just joshing you Randall," retorted Willie. "She's as sweet a lady as I have ever known and makes some of the best biscuits I've ever put in my mouth."

They stayed there about 12 days, when they got word that more of the Regiment had died and some more of Company I had succumbed to illness. So far nobody in their company had been wounded, all of the

17

casualties were those of disease, everything from pneumonia to mumps and measles and dysentery and some even typhoid fever.

On May 21, 1862, their brigade was placed in the division commanded by General Daniel Harvey Hill. He was the brother in law of "Stonewall Jackson". General Hill was known to be a fighter like his brother-in-law. Colonel Levi Smith, who was the regiment's Colonel, commanding, was directed to Seven Pines, Virginia and ordered to take a position to the right of the railroad that went through town. They were on the right of Colonel Jenkins' South Carolina sharpshooters. The battle raged hot on the South side of the railroad that day. Willie shot 30 of his 60 cartridges in the engagement, as they moved toward the two Yankee corps in their front. At the very end of the first day at Seven Pines, they helped Colonel Jenkins drive back the flanking federal force and push forward deeper than any of the Confederate units that day. Willie had perfected the "rebel yell." Randall was even getting the hang of it, although they had only been in two engagements before this day. This day was different, for they were in the hottest part of the battle on this fateful day.

When they rested that evening, Randall told Willie, "I ain't never imagined they were that many blue uniformed Yankees in Virginia. They just kept coming. There were lots of them fell and we sure licked them good today, didn't we, Willie?"

"We shore did, Randall, and if they know what's good for them they'll skedaddle on back to where they belong," remarked Willie, "Did you see all of them bayonets a-gleamin' in the sun today? I don't know how many soldiers it takes to make up a corps but it sure takes a passel."

"We better get to clean-in' these muskets or they might not shoot tomorrow," remarked Randall, as he placed the pot on the fire to heat the water to clean his musket. Willie joined him, and presently they were through with the gun cleaning and had oiled the guns down, in preparation for the next day. They took out the rations they had cooked that morning and began to chew on a hard piece of bacon to gain some nourishment.

When they were back home they would only kill hogs once a year on the coldest day. Everybody had to work in that procedure. First, they would scald the hog and scrape all the hair off the skin. Then they would begin to dismantle the hog, the choicest pieces for the smokehouse. They would take salt and rub it all over the hams. They would take the pork bellies and salt them down good and hang them in the smokehouse also. This is where they would get their bacon. They would dismantle that hog to the point where as some old folks would say "the only thing that wasn't used from the hog was the oink." They would make sausages and place them in the smokehouse. They would eat a little bit of fresh pork that day and the next. The bacon that they put in the smokehouse would have to last all year long so they didn't eat it every day. In General Johnston's Army they ate pork regularly and mostly it was bacon or salt pork. Randall looked like he was even gaining weight off all the cornbread and bacon he was eating in the Army.

They heard that Colonel Smith was wounded early in the fight but did not leave the field until the regiment and the brigade were relieved. The next day the battle was on again, and the Twenty-seventh was in the middle of the hot work. Late in the afternoon, the Twenty-seventh Georgia and Colonel Jenkin's Regiment ran the Yankees off the center of their position and pursued them all the way to their works. Captain Lee, of the Appling Grays, was killed outright, leading the charge that afternoon. Lieutenant Colonel Zachary had replaced Colonel Smith and was pressing the troops forward. Willie and Randall were side-by-side, bayonets fixed on their muskets yelling and screaming while charging and watching the blue coated Yankees as they retreated. Looking to the left they saw the color bearer of the Twenty-seventh Georgia go down holding the flag. General Anderson, who was close behind them, reached down and grabbed the flag up, riding upon his horse to rally the boys by waving the banner. When Randall saw this, it just made him want to fight more and press forward harder. Willie looked and there was Adjutant Gardner fighting like a banshee. There's no telling how many Yankees he took down that day. He was solid as a rock, and the men responded to his gallantry and bravery. As they rested that night on the breastworks, they learned that Captain Bacon had gone down and his wound was mortal. As they laid there on the ground trying to gain some rest, they learned that five of their men had been killed in the battle. They also learned that one of their sergeants, Sergeant Baxley and one of their corporals, their friend

Corporal Beecher were wounded along with three privates. One of those privates had been just to the right of Willie and Randall when he was hit. Randall had twisted his ankle charging up the embankment, but he would be all right.

Captain Lee would be sorely missed because he was a brave leader and a good man. They elected another good man to become Captain, Elisha Duncan Graham. Alex Johnson was elected second Lieutenant to fill Captain Graham's place. They went back in the camp to rest and recover, since the Yankees had retreated. Little did they know that in less than a month they would fight for seven days around the city of Richmond and would end up in some of the hottest battles that went on that week. Right now they needed to catch a breath. They needed to heal up things like Randall's ankle. Willie was just tired. He had done a lot of running and shooting and screaming and yelling and although he didn't know how many Yankees he took down that day. He saw some fall up close and personal, especially the blonde headed Sergeant with the beard whose cap and ball revolver had snapped as he pointed it at Willie's head. Willie's Springfield didn't snap and at that close a range, the Yankee sergeant flew back into his men. The Twenty-seventh had suffered quite a few casualties but they had given better than they received.

"That ankle gonna be all right Randall?" Willy inquired that night as they sat on the ground trying to regain their strength, after the strenuous day of fighting Yankees.

Randall answered him with a grimace saying, "It is pretty sore, but I've hurt it worse before running into the River swamp stepping on some of those roots of the Tupelo trees."

As Willie lay down, unrolling his blanket and laying it over him, he informed Randall, "Get you some rest tonight. Maybe that ankle will be better in the mornin'. I need some myself. I'm right tired and worn out. This has been a rough last two days but I believe the worst part was screaming at the top of my lungs trying to make my rebel yell louder than yours is."

Randall chuckled at this, as he too unrolled his blanket so he could get some sleep. He pondered how he and the best friend he had in this world had come this far and already been through so much.

On 24 June 1862, Colonel Alfred H. Colquitt, who had been Colonel of the Sixth Georgia was given the command of the brigade. Upon hearing that General Johnston had been wounded in the battle, all the troops were concerned for his health. They were worried about his leadership not being there anymore. The buzz went around the camp, though, on the next day that the command of the Army of Northern Virginia had been turned over to General Robert E. Lee. Everyone had heard about General Lee. General Lee had been the only man to ever go through West Point without a single demerit. Almost everyone in the South knew that he had been offered command of the whole United States Army and resigned his commission in the United States Army saying "Virginia is my mother. I cannot draw my sword against my mother." General Lee had not really had any command assignments for the Confederacy. His job had been assisting President Davis, more of an administrative role. Although he had been involved in squelching the rebellion of John Brown at the Harper's Ferry arsenal and had an exemplary service record in the Mexican War, no one knew at the time what kind of Commanding General he would be.

As they sat around the campfire and warmed that night, Willie and Randall talked over the politics of the Confederacy. Although they were young, they had seen a lot and knew a lot more than they had a few months ago. They had "Seen the Elephant" (a saying to denote that they had been in all-out battle) at Seven Pines. They had been in the midst of a major fight in the hottest place of that fight. They had fought like men. No longer were they 16-year-old boys, now they were 16-year-old fightin' men in the Army of Northern Virginia and were defending their country against an invading enemy wearing blue.

"When you think we gonna fight again Willie?" said Randall as he organized his accouterments and his haversack.

"Don't know, but I'm ready," Willie retorted. They were both growing beards as best a 16-year-old can. That was a lot easier than trying to shave. You cut yourself a whole lot less.

"Soldiers shore do a lot of drillin' and marchin' around, don't they?" piped Randall. 'I don't guess we could stand and fight all the time and we might not have enough men to go around if we did."

To which Willie replied, "Yeah we sure lost a lot of good boys and men the other day, didn't we. It was a really hot fight there for a while. I 'bout got plum tuckered out chasing them Yankees."

"My ankle still bothers me a mite but I read that if you would wrap an old rag round it so it can stay warm and then maybe it will be better. The sergeant said he would give me some horse liniment if I wanted it. That stuff stinks! I never would be able to go to sleep if I had that stinking mess on my ankle." said Randall.

"Neither would I," said Willie. "We smell bad enough as it is. I'll be glad when we get close to a river where I can take a bath or at least a swim and get some of this grime off of me."

"You always did like swimming in the "whirl hole" at Ten Mile Creek, didn't you?" answered Randall. "I would kind a be delighted to and wouldn't mind if they give me a chance for a little swim, even for a skinny dip if I could get away from people. That's about impossible around here. There are people everywhere. Did you taste some of that coffee that the corporal had the other day? He took it off a dead Yankee. He called it Mister Lincoln's coffee. That stuff was good. It was better than that we bought from the sutler, and it sure beats parching corn and boiling it, trying to make something to drink."

"I would just like to have some cool, clean, sparkling spring water from that spring that we found, when we were fishing at Rock Lake that time. It was the best water I ever drank. This stuff is muddy and I saw something swimming in mine the other day, when I dipped it out of the Chickahominy River," said Willie.

"Well we better get us some sleep, no telling when them blue bellies will come back. We need to be ready for 'em when they come, so we can send them back again, running for their lives." With that Randall began to scamper into the "dog tent" that the boys called home. Willie was not far behind him. Although the ground was hard, it didn't take much to get to sleep when you were tired as they usually were after drilling and marching.

The next morning, they were aroused early and were told to strike the tents. They gathered up their possibles, got on all their accouterments and took their place in line. They marched toward a little town named Mechanicsville, and about 1:30 in the afternoon they arrived.

The next morning, General Lee had his troops massing. They caught a glimpse of General Daniel Harvey Hill in the road as he talked with Colonel Colquitt and his aides. Colonel Colquitt quickly called in all of the colonels and lieutenant colonels from the regiments of his brigade and began to give them instructions. At first they were held in the reserve and they could hear the cannon and musketry. They knew that General A. P. Hill was engaged with the enemy to the northeast of them. It wasn't long before General Daniel Harvey Hill's division was sent forward to support. They were at a place somebody called Beaver Dam Creek near Mechanicsville, Virginia.

The fight got hot. Willie, with Randall to his left, was firing and loading his musket just as fast as he could. Willie looked around, and the only other Regiment there alongside the Twenty-seventh was the Sixth Georgia, which were one of the other regiments of their brigade. Then, the Sixth Georgia was moved off to the left and the Twenty-seventh was there by themselves, trying to hold that position. They stayed there for some time without any assistance from anybody else, and Willie looked to his right and noted that the Beecher brothers were both down on the ground wounded. Suddenly firing was coming from behind them. They turned and looked and could see the colors of the Sixty-first Georgia of

Lawton's Brigade and they were firing upon them. The Color Sergeant picked up the banner of the Twenty-seventh and began to wave it so that the men of the Sixty-first could see that they were firing upon not the enemy, but upon fellow Georgians.

When the Sixty-first soldiers recognized the Twenty-seventh Georgia flag, they ceased firing to the regiment's relief. The Yankees began to retreat, and once again the rebel yell was heard as the Georgians pressed them. They were heading toward a place called Cold Harbor, and the Regiment was on the side near Boatswain Swamp.

Late that afternoon, the order came down the line to charge and Willie and Randall were wading knee-deep through that Swamp to try to gain an advantage on the Yankee line. When they finally broke out of the swamp on the other side, they found themselves on the flank of General Porter's federal division. Randall was running, screaming like a banshee, he had a strange rebel yell, going toward the enemy line. They rushed so fast that the enemy broke ranks. They pressed them on until dark came and the action stopped.

Sitting with his back to a pine tree, Randall said, "Willie, did you see them Yankees a running. They looked like turkeys in the Altamaha Swamp. I think we surprised them when we popped out of that old swamp, but they didn't know that they were facing old swampers from South Georgia, did they?"

"No, and they left their dead and wounded on the field", replied Willie. "Sometimes I feel sorry for them old wounded boys laying out there, although the dead ones don't need anything else now but burying. I'm glad I need more than burying. Are them Beecher brothers okay? I saw them go down when they got hit."

"This was a tough fight today but I believe we got the best of them," exclaimed Randall. "I wonder what tomorrow will bring?"

Tomorrow brought Gaines Mill, where the fight was hot again. Colquitt's brigade, including the Twenty-seventh Georgia continued to drive the enemy back. They fought at Savage Station and then at White Oak Swamp. On June 31, 1862 they were again engaged on the Willis Church Road. As they came upon a place called Malvern Hill, Colquitt's Brigade and Hill's Division were in the center of the attack. They charged right into the teeth of the Yankee artillery, perched on the top of the little hill. The Yankees switched over from firing exploding shells to shooting double canister, which was like a great big shotgun of grapeshot. Many men went down in the lines as they charged, but at the end of the day, Willie and Randall lay on the ground worn completely out but the Yankees had pulled back. Old Marse Robert had done that.

The Seven Days around Richmond battle was over and they had pushed them Yankees back and as somebody said, completely off the peninsula back in the Yankeedom. As they lay there panting they knew lots of their fellows in the Twenty-seventh had gone down. They knew that some of them were dead and many others were wounded. So far Willie and Randall had only suffered minor scratches and bruises and of course Randall's sprained ankle awhile back. The weather was hot there on July 1, 1862 and their uniforms were soaked with sweat. As they sat there, Willie noticed that he had torn his pants leg, most likely back in White Oak Swamp, cause there were a couple of times he got hung up pretty bad in the cat-claw briars. Word came down the line that Captain Gardner had been wounded. There was no braver man in the regiment than him.

"I believe that Captain Gardner would stand toe-to-toe with the devil without fear," exclaimed Willie.

"Yep. He'd probably whup him too!" replied Randall.

Willie reached in his haversack and pulled out a "housewife" that he had bought off a sutler at Camp Pickens. This "housewife" was a little packet that contained needles, thread, buttons and little patches of cloth that could be used in repairing your uniform. Willie wished he had learned better from his mother how to sew, but he eventually got that tear tied down on his pants. It wasn't pretty but it was back together. Placing the housewife back in the haversack, he retrieved a piece of bacon and some cornbread that was not but two days old and began to chew on it for nourishment. Although during a lull in the swamp, he did grab a handful of grapes and wolfed them down during the heat of the battle. This would be all he had eaten that day. The water in his canteen tasted awful. He had gotten it out of the flowing well, and it tasted about like the gunpowder smelled, but it was all he had.

The next day, they were still encamped there at Richmond and word reached them that Elisha, one of their friends from out near the river, had died in Chimborazo Hospital and was buried in a cemetery, they had started near the hospital. He died from typhoid fever. Willie had never heard of that before, but he knew of several folks that had died from it since he arrived in Virginia. Randall had the fire going and raked some coals over to the side, placing the spider on it, laying pieces of bacon in there to cook. Willie loved bacon, but he had no idea that about all soldiers ate was bacon and cornbread. He sure would like to have some of that sausage daddy used to make, when they would kill hogs in the winter. He also would like to have a mess of greens like his momma would cook up. He lay there and closed his eyes and reminisced about the days growing up on the farm. He had always worked hard, since he was eight or nine. He chopped wood and plowed the ox. He still had lots of free time to scamper in the river swamp. He had become a good shot as a young boy. His mother would allow him to go into the swamp with his granddaddy's old .36 caliber flintlock to hunt squirrels. After his grandmother had complained about him shooting the squirrels in the shoulder and messing up the meat, he had become an excellent shot and would only head shoot a squirrel so as to not damage any usable meat. He was a good fisherman too and had "cooned" many a catfish out from under the roots of the trees in the sloughs of the river and in Ten Mile Creek. He was good at bringing meat for the table even as a young lad. He kind of missed that now that he was so far away from home. He often wondered how everybody was, since he had not received any letters lately. Or at least they may not have caught up with him yet, although he continued to write home, religiously.

They stayed encamped near Richmond until mid-August, when Willie heard that his cousin Peter Kemp had died in Chimborazo Hospital

26

with typhoid fever, too. Willie guessed that he'd probably be buried in that same cemetery. As he lay there thinking about that, the Sergeant came by and informed them that they were again to "strike the tent" and prepare to move. Randall and Willie quickly took down their dog tent, folding it up neatly and rolling up their blankets and loaded everything in their haversacks. They had not completed that task but just a few minutes, when orders were given for them to fall into line and into rank. They scurried over and took their place anxious to see what was going on. Was the enemy close by? Where they gonna fight again that day? All of these questions swirled in their heads as they took up a line of march toward a train that was waiting. They piled into the cars of the train, and when everyone was on the train, it lurched forward. After what seemed to be a long time, the train came to a halt at Orange Court House where they disembarked from the train cars. They set up camp and stayed there for about a week, until orders came for them to move out.

They took a line of march North toward Fairfax County, Virginia. They were told that they were going to join General Lee and General Jackson near Fairfax, Virginia. Finally, on the third of September, the Regiment arrived in Fairfax. They set up camp and stayed there three days, until General Lee and the other high-ranking officers of the Confederacy could plan what they were going to do. Word came back to the ranks that they were going into Maryland. That was Yankeedom! Why were they goin' there?

Once while they were drilling, General Lee rode up on a magnificent gray horse. Some said his name was Traveler. Willie had never seen a finer looking officer that General Lee. He sat a horse better than anyone he had ever seen, erect and stately. His uniform was clean and perfect. His gray hair and beard looked outstanding. He was an inspiration to his men just as they caught a glimpse of him coming by. General Lee's men would have followed him into hell if he asked them to.

General Lee

Chapter Three: South Mountain and the Bloodiest Day

On the early morning of September 4, they were ordered to cook three days rations and prepare to move out. "Cook three days rations" usually meant they were getting ready to fight. Willie and Randall cooked up all the bacon they could get their hands on and made some cornbread hoe cakes, because they knew there would be no time for any cooking in the next few days. After a few days they moved to Leesburg and then to Frederick, Maryland. They marched over the gap on South Mountain toward Boonsboro, Maryland on the National Pike. But on September 13, the brigade was quickly marched back over the South Mountain pass to the Mountain House, which was toll station where folks had to pay the toll when they used the Pike. Lee's army didn't have to pay a toll. They were told by Captain Graham that their job was to protect Turner's Gap and to keep the federal army from advancing toward Lee's main army, which he had split. Stonewall Jackson had taken part of the army toward Harper's Ferry, for there were a good number of federal troops stationed there. Harper's Ferry was the site of a federal arsenal, that the Confederates had taken early in the war, and had moved all of the equipment to make "the Harpers Ferry musket" to Richmond. It was also the site that John Brown, the abolitionist, had seized before the war, and General Lee who was at that time Colonel Robert E. Lee of the United States Army, had gone there with troops and put down the uprising. John Brown was later hanged for his treason.

As the brigade marched to what was the military crest of the hill, they took up a position with the Twenty-eight and the Twenty-third Georgia to the left of the Pike, in a heavy wooded area. They were positioned with the Sixth Georgia, Twenty-seventh Georgia and the Thirteenth Alabama to the right. Company H and Company I of the Twenty-seventh Georgia were detached and placed directly to the right of the National Pike. Directly in front of the two companies was a stone wall around a little area that had been tended for farming. As they were crouching behind the fence trying to see what was coming up the mountain, they wondered what would happen next. The view from that Mountain was awesome. Willie had never seen a mountain before joining up, and this was the first time he'd ever been on top of one. The view was unobscured for miles. As they looked down the mountain, they could see the blue of the federal uniforms in formation, but they were not moving forward yet.

"When do you think they'll come? How many do you think there are? Will we be able to hold this position?" Randall was full of questions.

Willie was too. "I don't know, but I'm glad we got this little stone wall in front of us, I believe it'll stop a mini ball."

"Do you reckon it'll stop a cannonball?" remarked Randall.

All Willie could say was, "I sure hope so, cause I bet they got plenty of 'em."

"When they start firing them Parrot guns we better hunker down low because them is some bad boys," piped Randall.

The two slept side-by-side that night behind the wall, in full anticipation of what the next day might bring. The ground was hard, and the farmer hadn't gotten all of the rocks out of the ground, so it was difficult to get in a comfortable position. Willie must've stayed awake until after midnight from a combination of pain from the rocks, and in anticipation of what could happen tomorrow

The next morning they came. At first, during the day, it was just light skirmishing, as the Yankees would send skirmishers out to locate the Confederate positions. Twenty-five or thirty skirmishers would come up in different groups in their front and fire upon them. When they had a good shot, they would return fire. Willie spotted an officer with his sword drawn directing the troops forward. He drew a bead and squeezed the trigger, watching the officer tumble down the mountain. The troops with him were in disorder after they didn't have a leader anymore. Some of his friends in the company had told him that he had become a sharpshooter, because he was the best shot in the company. They held that position until late in the afternoon, when a brigade of Yankees brought forth a full-fledged attack on their position. Cannons would fire from both sides and ordinance would explode around them, but Willie and Randall stayed behind that stone wall that mini balls couldn't penetrate. Every once in a while, you would hear the whine as a mini ball ricocheted off that wall. The attack was hot and heavy but the brigade drove them back. When they did, they could hear General Longstreet's staff at the Mountain House let out a cheer.

"Hooray for Georgia! Georgia is having a good fight." They shouted.

The Yankee brigade tried to make a second charge. Again, the fire was hot and heavy as the Twenty-seventh Georgians and the others unleashed murderous volleys upon them. They fell back once more, and once more the cheer came from the Mountain House.

A third time the Yankees tried to make it back up that mountain, and once again they were thrown back by the gallant Confederates of Colquitt's Brigade. To the right Willie thought that hell had broken loose toward Fox's Gap and Crampton's Gap, where other units were trying to hold off the Yankee advance. He later found out that Crampton's had been overrun and that General Garland had been killed. Word was also passed down the line that Captain Graham had been wounded in this action at Turner's Gap. The Yankees had kept coming, but on every occasion they were thrown back. The fire from the muskets would sound like a sheet tearing. A ripping sound quickly followed by boys in blue falling to the ground.

That night they withdrew across South Mountain and marched by way of Boonsboro toward a little town named Sharpsburg. They withdrew to Sharpsburg and then down to the North Shore of the Potomac across from Shepherdsville, Virginia. They stayed there for a little over a day and cooked three days rations once more. They heard that General Jackson had captured 12,500 federals at Harper's Ferry and was on the way to join them. On the morning of September 17, they were moved into a position in a sunken road near Sharpsburg. They were on the very left side of the sunken road at daylight. They lay there in the predawn darkness wondering what this day would bring.

"Can you see anything out there, Willie," Randall asked. "I can't make out a thing."

"I can't either, but I sure hear a lot of marchin', horses and such," retorted Willie. "It must be a bunch of them over there to be making that much noise."

John who was over next to Randall said, "You wonder on days like today whether you'll still be here, when the sun goes down, amongst the living or if you'll be laying out there on that field waiting to be placed in a hole somebody's dug in the ground or even worse being eaten by them buzzards."

"We can't be worrying about that, John," said Randall. "We just need to go out and do the best we can and hopefully teach them Yankees to leave the Confederacy alone. Live and let live I say, if we can only teach them that."

"All right boys get up, we're moving out," said the sergeant as he came by.

It was just cracking morning when they began to form up, getting ready to march. They marched straight out of the sunken road and joined up with Hood's Texicans on their right, at the edge of a cornfield. They begin to move forward in the cornfield about seven thirty in the morning and started to meet some resistance in their front. Colquitt's brigade was in the center of three of General Daniel Harvey Hill's brigades with Ripley's to the left and Garland's to the right. Both had been engaged at South Mountain, and Colonel McRae was leading in the place of the dead General Garland.

As they advanced across the cornfield, they began to push the Yankees out of the far end of the cornfield. They were on the far right of the advance and the Sixth Georgia along with the Twenty-seventh really began to push the enemy back into the woods. On their right, Colonel McRae's men fell back for some unknown reason, and on the left, the brigade was not moving up fast as Colquitt's. Colquitt's Brigade began to do a wheel left maneuver with the Sixth Georgia on the far right, the Twenty-seventh Georgia next to them. Both Regiments were in the most advanced positions.

They had the Yankees on the run again and were pressing the issue forward. Suddenly, on the right of the Sixth Georgia a Yankee brigade came out of the East Woods, and their men began to fire into the flank of the Sixth Georgia, doing what is called enfilade firing. Those brave boys of the Sixth started to go down. As they fell, it cleared the way for mini balls to make it into the flank of the Twenty-seventh. Willie heard a thud and saw Sergeant Milliken, his cousin, go down. The Sergeant's friend, Blue Sapp, grabbed him by the arm and drug him up beside a tree, leaning him against the trunk of the tree. Then all of a sudden, Yankees were everywhere. They had their bayonets fixed and so did the boys of the Twenty-seventh. People were fighting everywhere hand-to-hand,

33

clubbing with the butts of muskets and bayonetting was going on everywhere.

Willie felt a sharp pain on the right side of his head. The impact took him to his knees. He looked up, and there was a large Yankee in blue poised to ram his bayonet in him. Willy quickly swept his Springfield at the knees of the attacker, cutting his legs from under him and plunging his own bayonet into the man's chest. Quickly withdrawing it, he looked for the next attacker to combat.

After much too long, the brigade began to withdraw. They withdrew all the way back to that sunken road again. There they took up the position they had occupied earlier in the morning. For three hours the Yankees would attack that sunken road time after time. For three hours the Confederates would unleash deadly volleys of fire into what was seen to be a sea of blue. Willie could only see the colors of the Yankees to start with, as they came up on the rise, just in their front. Then the columns would pour over the top of that little rise. When they did the sergeant down from them would yell, "Aim low boys, aim low." They just kept coming. Wave after wave they attacked. All Willie and Randall could do was load and fire. Willie heard a thud and looked to see John go down in the sunken road. He was atop two more soldiers who had gone down before him. In one of the lulls, he looked to his right where the hottest of the battle was occurring and wondered if the day would ever end. The Sixty-first Georgia was in position there, and he could see that Lawton's brigade, of which they were a part, was in the sunken road. He thought he saw Colonel Gordon, a valiant soldier that he had seen once and had heard lots about. Gordon was a regimental commander.

After about three hours' time, the order was given to withdraw. Willie could not believe his eyes, as they pulled out of that sunken road, at his Confederate comrades piled on top of one another all up and down. That place would later be dubbed "Bloody Lane". What was left of the Twenty-seventh Georgia withdrew back toward the Potomac River and fought alongside General A. P. Hill's troops on the Hagerstown Pike at Dunkard Church later that day. This was the third time that they had been in pitched battle already that day. They had heard cannonade and musketry over toward the stone bridge they had crossed the day before but were not sure what was going on there.

After that action was over and dark had come, Willie looked around for Randall, finding him on the ground with his thigh bleeding. He helped him up. With Randall's arm over his shoulder they moved back toward the Potomac River. The next morning, before they crossed the river, he had tied a bandage on Randall's leg, but it was still bleeding badly so he got him to the surgeon. The surgeon poured turpentine on it and said that it had passed through without hitting the bone, so Randall would not lose his leg unless infection set up in the wound. Gangrene was the worst fear of the wounded man. Willie had heard how some men had saved their legs because the blow flies had laid eggs in the wound and the maggots ate the putrefying flesh. That sounded nasty but he'd rather have maggots than lose a leg and he knew Randall would too.

A mini ball had grazed Willie's shoulder but had not hurt him badly and he had easily stopped the bleeding from the slight wound. He was thinking about how badly he sewed and what his jacket would look like after patching that hole.

"This hurts a lot worse than a sprained ankle," stated Randall.

"Looks lots worse too," answered Willie.

"Are you hit too?" asked Randall.

"Yeah. It ain't too bad though. I've had worse from the cat claw briars in the river swamp," joked Willie.

"This was by far the worst fight we've ever been in," said Randall. "I don't see how a fight could get any worser than this one, Willie."

"You sure are right. It is a pity how many men we left in that sunken road. They were piled 3 deep and 4 deep in places. Them Yankees

35

kept a coming. No matter how many we shot down, there were more boys in blue in our front," remarked Randall.

"I didn't keep count of how many shots I fired, but I do know that I fired all 60 that I started with before the ordinance sergeant's man gave me more in that sunken road," stated Willie.

"I know you kidded me way back then when we didn't have any muskets about having to wrestle in this fight against these Yankees, but you know we were about to that at the end of that cornfield this morning. You see Sergeant Ben go down? He was hit in the leg, but I don't know what happened to him. Yankees probably got him now, and maybe their surgeons are doctoring on him. I'm gonna miss him 'cause he was a fine sergeant," Randall said as he pushed his hand on his thigh where his wound was. Both were lucky to still be alive as many mini balls as flew through the air on this day and very many exploding artillery shells hit all around them.

Just then the ambulance wagon came by and Willie helped load Randall into the back of it. Randall made him promise that he would come check on him. Willie said that he would because the food would be better there than at the company encampment. Willy watched as the ambulance pulled away, thinking that had that mini ball hit an inch further over to the right, Randall would have lost his leg. A soldier just did not realize the danger he was in while he was in the midst of battle. All he can think about at that time is kill or be killed.

Company I had lost several men, killed, wounded and captured. Among them was their sergeant, who had led them in the battle. They had lost Colonel Levi Smith to a Yankee mini ball. Someone said that all but one of the field grade officers in the Twenty-seventh had gone down with half of them being killed.

This was the worst battle that Willie had ever been in. He had lost friends and had almost lost his best friend. He went over by the makeshift hospital area to check on Randall and asked the surgeon if there was anything he could do. The surgeon told him to wash his hands, put down his accouterments and that he could help tend to these men that were wounded. Willie never had much experience at doctoring or nursing, but he guessed it was time to learn. He mostly just took canteens to the men to satisfy their thirst and check to make sure they were not bleeding too badly. When he found one that was bleeding more, he would notify the surgeon who would presently look at him.

Over the next few days, some would succumb to their wounds. Randall seemed to be getting better especially when they brought him some boiled beef to eat. Randall had developed a real liking to boiled beef and he especially liked the broth. He said it was soothing as it went down his gullet. The bleeding had stopped, and he thanked Willie for helping him to get out of there, because he didn't think he wanted to be a prisoner of war. He'd already heard enough stories of how bad the Yankees treated their prisoners of war and how some of them had eaten rats for protein because even though the Yankees had plenty of food they would withhold it from the Confederate prisoners for spite. They called them names like Reb, Seccesh and other demeaning names. Willie was quite pleased that Randall had not been taken prisoner also. He didn't want to be without his best friend. Not off in the foreign land of Maryland. They were glad to be back on the Virginia side of the river. September 17, 1862 was the bloodiest, worst day that Willie and Randall would ever see or anyone else in American history. They lost more friends and saw more carnage than any boys that age should have.

The Regiment marched on to Martinsburg and then to Bunker Hill. As soon as all of the wounded had been removed they tore up the railroad track between Winchester and Harper's Ferry. Company I had to hold elections after that battle to replace the officers and noncommissioned officers that were either lost or put out of commission. Lieutenant Colonel Zachary from Henry County was elevated to the position of Colonel, and Willie was elected third corporal, a position he really didn't want, but the rest of the fellows in the company wanted him and thought that he deserved it. So that was all right with him. Randall was so tickled that Willie was a now a corporal that he was beside himself. Hobbling around on that bad leg, he was telling everyone how his buddy was a new corporal.

It was a good thing that Randall's leg healed quickly, because between the 15th and 20th of November they marched about 20 miles a day passing Guinea Station going through Orange Court House and arrived somewhere near Port Royal on the Rappahannock River. The weather was turning cold and it was beginning to snow some in Northern Virginia. Willie and Randall had never seen snow, not down in South Georgia. This was their second winter in Virginia and they had now seen plenty of it. Goodness would they have stories to tell the people back in Appling County when they got home, if they did.

Their Regiment was down from over 1000 men in the 10 companies that they started with to about 600 ready for duty. If the rest of the wounded ones healed up they might have something over 700. Some of the men's shoes had worn out, and they made sandals out of rawhide. They didn't work well in the snow because they would not keep your foot warm, but they did work better than going barefoot which Willie had seen. He remembered some soldiers walking barefoot in the snow and leaving bloody footprints. That sight would remain in his brain for the rest of his life along with what went on at Sharpsburg. There were times when supplies ran short, and this was one of them. Some men spoke of boiling their shoes and eating them, but Willie thought surely they must be kidding. He was hungry though and had not really had enough to eat the last several days. There were no crops in the field during the winter, so the only grain that they could get would have to be that the local farmers gave them or that which was conscripted by the Confederate government. Willy thought how good it would be just to have a squirrel to roast over the fire like they used to back home, when he and Randall would camp in the river swamp, or to have a bream battered in cornmeal and fried in lard. That just made him miss home more to think about it. His mind would wander and think about his younger days, as he looked across the fire at his best friend, Randall. He would never have another friend that good and he could not afford to lose him in this war.

Willie and Randall had often pulled picket duty together. They had spent many a dark, cold night, trying to stay awake and look out for the enemy. Although the cavalry did most of the reconnoitering to discover enemy activity, the pickets also served as an early warning system, so that the encampment of troops would not be surprised by an enemy attack. This night they were surprised by horses' hoof beats.

As the riders neared them, Randall called out, "halt. Who are you? Identify yourself, sir".

The answer came. "Captain Mosby, 43rd Battalion Virginia Cavalry." Mosby emerged from the darkness with three other riders. They had heard of Mosby. He was the one that had led Jeb Stuart around McClellan, while they were fighting the Seven days battles around Richmond.

"Would one of you boys show me to your commanding officer's headquarters tent?" said Mosby in a voice that exuded authority.

"Sure will, Captain," Randall snapped to attention and saluted the captain. He began to lead Mosby toward the encampment. About 20 minutes later he returned all exuberant.

"Willie, do you believe that? I have heard a lot about Mosby and his Rangers. They have been terrorizing the Yankees in the five counties of Northern Virginia. They even call those counties Mosby's Confederacy. The Yankees can't move without Mosby or some of his men knowing just where they are and just where they are going," said Randall with the excitement still in his eyes. "If we had more like him, the war would probably already be over, and the Yankees would be leaving us alone."

"I've heard a lot about him too. I understand to be in his cavalry unit that you have to have your own horse and at least two of them Colt's pistols with two extra loaded cylinders. But he would prefer you have two on your belt and two on your saddle in pommel holsters. He also won't let them carry a sword. Somebody said that he had told them that a sword made too much noise when you rode and was only fitting for barbecuing a piece of meat over the fire. Did you notice that about the three boys that

39

rode alongside him? No sabers and four pistols. I bet they could do damage for 24 shots, when they ride into the flank of a column of Yankee cavalry."

Randall sadly retorted, "I guess we are just destined to be foot soldiers. No horse. I do have that pistol I took off that Yankee officer at Cold Harbor but don't have no balls to put in it, so it just sits in my haversack. I'd like to be a cavalryman and ride with somebody like Mosby. I bet all the girls like Mosby's men."

"I reckon we are going to just be infantry," replied Willie. "But some girls like foot soldiers too."

"If I make it through this war, I'm gonna buy me a fine ridin' horse one day. I might even get a gray one like Traveler," mused Randall.

The next day they found out what Mosby had reported to their commander. They again struck camp and took up a line of march toward a town called Fredericksburg. They arrived there and on the 13th of December. Colquitt's Brigade was placed on Lee's far right on high ground. From the top of the ridge, they could see the Yankees cross in the river on pontoon bridges. They were just pouring across that river like a blue tide coming in. Colquitt's Brigade was to demonstrate on that far right position to attract the attention of the Yankees and to make them think that the attack was coming from that side. Pelham had his cannons down there and fired several volleys into the Yankees. What the Yankees didn't know was that General Lee was on Marye's Heights waiting for them to come that way. When the Yankees would get into the killing zone, the men in gray would unleash death dealing volleys into them. They were falling in piles in their front. The Yankee general kept sending them. They kept falling. They had heard that General Lee once said that it is good that war is so terrible lest we begin to love it. This was a terrible day for those Yankees. Although the Twenty-seventh didn't draw trigger, they watched an amazing defense of those heights. Finally, the Yankees withdrew while there were still some left. Willie later discovered that the Yankee general was Burnside, the same one that sent his men over that stone bridge near Sharpsburg where those Georgia boys held the high ground and took a deadly toll of Yankees that day. Now he was in command of the whole Army of the Potomac. He did not act any smarter now than he did in Sharpsburg.

Word came to the men that Colonel Colquitt had been promoted to General Colquitt. Some were even calling him the "Rock of South Mountain" for the brigade's stout defense of Turner's Gap. He was an electrifying general and all his boys were proud to follow him. He sat on that horse at Sharpsburg with mini balls whizzing by him and cannon balls exploding around him and never showed fear. That was inspiring to the troops of his brigade, and most of those boys would've followed him almost anywhere.

After the battle of Fredericksburg, the brigade went into winter quarters close by. Willie and Randall built a little shelter in which they could stay warm and dry. They had enough tree boughs on the roof so that even the snow and rain could not get through. The sides were built with saplings, which they had lashed together. They could be fairly cozy in that thing when the weather outside was awful. Willie had gotten permission to go see if he could take some meat for the camp. He and Randall were given permission and they moved out into the Northern Virginia woods. Willie spotted a large Virginia whitetail buck and used all the skills he had honed in the Altamaha River swamp to get close enough for a shot. He raised his musket and dropped the buck with one shot. He and Randall dressed the deer and cut a sapling to carry it back to camp. When they arrived with their prize buck to camp all the boys cheered them. Captain Graham came out to meet them and praised them for their good work. The meat was split up amongst the company with Willie and Randall getting the choicest part, the tenderloin. They went back to their hut where Randall started up a fire of hardwood. When it began to coal up, he suspended the meat on sticks over the coals, sprinkling a bit of salt on it as it cooked. Willie put on some roasting corn kernels to make something that still only resembled coffee to drink with their feast. They ate that tenderloin, drank that imitation coffee and laid-back to relax. Several of their friends came by to thank them for getting meat for the camp. They were a little tired of salted meat, and the meat from the buck was really good to them.

They stayed in winter quarters so long, and the winter was so cold, that they burned up all of the available wood around them. Some farmer could grow corn here now where the forest used to stand. They had lots of time to think of home and six letters finally caught up to Willie from his mother. He read all six of them over and over again getting a little melancholy and thinking about home and about his mother, his father and his little sister. One of the letters from his mother said that his father was still in the Savannah-Charleston area and was in Company B of the Fifty-fourth Georgia Infantry, the Appling Volunteers. She told how the Yankees had blockaded Savannah and Charleston's ports. She also said that there were three companies of Appling Countians in the Savannah and Charleston area. She also told him how one of their neighbors, William Eason, was in the same company with his father. He was a real athlete, and he had been dared to jump over a canal in Savannah. He attempted it but didn't quite make it with his chest hitting the upper portion of the bank. The surgeons looked after him but in four or five days he died. They put his body on the Gulf and Atlantic railroad in Savannah and had taken him to Doctortown on the Altamaha River. His casket was then placed on a cannon caisson to be transported back to Appling County. They said that a Confederate officer mounted on a fine black steed had come before him to the community, and they were told that his body would soon be there. She also said that when his body arrived that everyone decided that he should be buried on the little plot of land off to the side of the little church called Bethel, where Willie and Randall used to attend. They decided that his grave would be the first there but that they would start a graveyard at that location for the people that attended the church and their families.

Willie wrote his mother a long letter that day and Randall wanted to read the letters, too. He hadn't had a letter in a while so Willie let him read them. Willie guessed that Randall was probably the closest thing to a brother that he would ever have, and he knew that Randall felt like family and would enjoy his mother's letters, too.

They got paid but didn't have anywhere to spend their money. They also were supplied with new uniforms and new brogans to wear. Randall got a new hat to replace the one he had lost at Sharpsburg. Randall sure was proud of the hat. It was a bummer and not a kepi like he had lost. Willie's new pants were lots better than those he had tried to sew together after the Seven Days Battle. His jacket was warmer than the one that he originally had been issued, which was a welcome thing to him.

Willie could write well, and several of the boys in the company that could not write would get him to write letters home for them. When they would get a letter from home, they would bring it to him to read to them. He enjoyed doing this for the boys, and because of it he also learned a lot more about what was going on in Appling County. At that time, it seemed that all of the able bodied boys and men between the ages of 16 and 45 were either off serving in either one of the four infantry companies from there or they were in Clinch's Fourth Cavalry. There were Appling Countians in both Company A and Company I, and their assignment was to patrol Southeast Georgia from the Altamaha River to the St. Mary's River, looking for Yankee activity and to keep them from sneaking into Georgia. There were some men over 45 who had horses and had become a part of John Mayer's Appling County Cavalry. Their job was to help out around the county where necessary. The only folks between 16 and 45 who weren't in the military were those who were either holding elected office or who were growing crops or beef for the Confederacy. Everyone was involved or dedicated in one way or another. A recruiter was sent back to Appling County to get more men enlisted into the Appling Grays. The only thing to choose from was the boys who had turned 16 since Willie and Randall left. Willie wished he could be the recruiter as he would like to see home again even if just for a little while. Corporals don't get to be recruiters. Usually it is a Lieutenant, maybe sometimes a Sergeant, but never a Corporal.

The winter of 1862 was awfully cold, colder than the two South Georgia boys had ever been. Sometimes South Georgia gets cold in January and February, but where they lived it never got this cold. There were times when they would wake up in the morning and there would be sheets of ice on their tents. Snow would stay on the ground for several days, while back home it rarely snowed and never stayed on the ground. If it did it would just be a little bit. It would not be inches deep like it is in Virginia in the winter. If you didn't bank your fire the night before you went to bed, it could be very difficult to get a fire started up in the morning, because there would be ice and snow on the firewood. The only good thing about drilling was that you would warm up. The rest of the time you tried to stay as close as you could to a fire or at least wrap your blanket around you as you were sitting around. The thing about the winter

43

was that food would not spoil easily. As the meat rations were given out, usually it would need to be cooked quickly so as to prevent spoilage. Most of the time, the meat would consist of some form of salted pork or smoked pork. Sometimes you would even have beef that you could boil. That way you had meat and a broth that was pleasant to drink and to warm your innards. Coffee was scarce, so the warm drink that was common around the campfire was corn that was poached, ground and boiled in water. It would pass as something warm other than water that had been warmed up. But on the rare occasion when coffee was available at the sutler's tent, Willie and Randall would treat themselves to what they heard referred to as Mister Lincoln's coffee. The landscape was bare in Virginia in the wintertime. There were no fruits, berries or even crops in the fields that they might partake of.

The snow finally quit falling and the weather began to warm, By April 1, it looked as though spring was here. The leaves were on the trees and the nights were not nearly as cold as they had been in December and January and also in February. They got word that Lieutenant Alfred Hall, the brother-in-law of the late Captain Osgood A. Lee, had died and his body had been shipped back to Georgia. He was the son of Seaborn Hall. Seaborn and James Latimer were the two Appling Countians that had gone to the secession convention in Milledgeville and voted for Georgia to secede from the union. Seaborn had stayed in the County due to his age and was a civic leader there while James Latimer had become Captain of the Appling Rangers, Company F, Forty-seventh Georgia Infantry.

The recruiter returned from Appling County with ten boys and gathered five more recruits while they were laid over in Atlanta, waiting for the train to Richmond. They did not bring the company up to full strength, but every new man helped the number. These men were quickly trained, equipped and indoctrinated into the everyday life in our company and regiment. Willie had to teach three how to shoot because they had never shot a rifle before. He taught them how to load by the nine's and all of the commands that they must follow. This was the Corporal's responsibility, and Willie was good at it. He drilled them every day intending to make good soldiers of them, and also he intended that they be the kind of soldiers that would hold their own in battle. They all responded well with a couple of them really excelling. One boy, Sam, who Willie had known from Appling County, who also lived near the

44

river, was an excellent shot. He could shoot almost as well as Willie, and Willie was the best in the Company. Randall had honed his shooting skills to the point where he could give Willie a run for his money.

They were sitting by the fire one night along with Sam and a couple of other guys talking about shooting Yankees. Randall wondered just how many Yankees he and Willie had killed and said so. Neither of them could count the number that had fallen to their muskets, but they agreed there had been several and Willie thought back about especially the Sergeant and the Lieutenant that he had taken out of commission. He could still see the Lieutenant rolling down South Mountain after he had shot him. He had also shot an artillery man at Sharpsburg as he was ramming the load home in the canon.

"I don't know how many we've killed Willie," said Randall, "but I'm sure we are good for several more before they get us." The new boys from Appling County looked at Randall strangely after he said that, because the fire of battle was in his eyes when he did so. Randall had become a fierce warrior, and no Yankee in his right mind would want to be in his front as he let out that bloodcurdling rebel yell of his and begin to charge.

"What does it feel like to shoot a Yankee?" inquired Sam.

Willie responded, "It don't feel real good but it would have to feel better than him shooting you."

"Yeah," stated Randall. "I've already been shot twice and neither one of them felt good. Matter of fact, I've still got a little bit of a limp from that last one. You'll find out soon enough, Sam."

"When do you reckon we'll fight again?" asked Sam.

"Soon enough! You don't really want to rush it. It will be after the weather begins to warm up cause Yankees and Rebs don't like to fight when it is cold," remarked Willie.

They were told by Willie and Randall the strange things they had seen and how the one general who was sitting on his horse when a solid cannonball struck the horse in the chest, passing all the way through and exiting in the rear of the horse with the general sitting atop. They brought him a fresh horse and he hopped up on it. They also remarked how General Robert E. Lee, General Stonewall Jackson and General Daniel Harvey Hill could sit atop their steeds totally ignoring shot, shell and mini ball as they led their men and looked upon the battle field to determine what their next move would be. These were the bravest men Willie had ever seen. They not only were brave but they were good men too, all three were good Christian men. Once when Willie was sent as a courier with a message for General Lee's headquarters, he arrived to find General Lee on his knees in prayer. Out in the open! Where everyone could see! It was obvious that this man was not ashamed of his Christian beliefs. Everyone knew that General Stonewall Jackson had begun a Sunday school in Lexington, Virginia for the children of the slaves. It was good to be led by people who were in touch with the Lord.

Word came to again strike the camp. On April 27, 1863 the brigade took up a line of march toward Chancellorsville, Virginia and arrived there the next day late in the afternoon. On the following day, April 29th, they were engaged with the enemy near the Wilderness Church. They fought hard all day long. Willie and Randall both almost emptied their cartridge pouches. They resupplied them and were ready for the next day's fighting again around Wilderness Church. They fought hard there on the second day. The casualties were minor for the regiment on those two days. They were then called to march. They were going with Stonewall Jackson to attempt to flank the enemy. There was one thing for sure about Jackson's men, they could march. They weren't called "Jackson's Foot Cavalry" for nothing. They could easily march 20 miles a day. Jackson's troops were taking the plank road to see if we could turn the enemy's right. This battle continued on and was waged fiercely. They turned the enemy's right flank and began moving to roll them up. Colquitt's brigade was on the far right of the flanking movement. Before dark on the first day, General Colquitt's scouts informed him of enemy movement to our right. Colquitt checked his progress to ensure that he did not have a repeat of the cornfield at Sharpsburg. As he did that the remainder of the flanking movement, which was all to his left began to check. The fighting ended that day. That night General Jackson and a party went out to reconnoiter the enemy's position. Upon turning back to the Confederate lines the pickets of a South Carolina unit mistook them for an enemy force and fired upon them, wounding the general in his arm. He was rushed to the surgeons who eventually had to amputate that arm.

General Robert E. Lee was quoted as saying, "General Jackson has lost his left arm but I have lost my right." A few days later General Jackson would "cross over the River and rest in the shade."

This was a terrible loss for the Confederacy. They had lost one of the best generals that ever led troops, one of the best tacticians ever and one of the most inspiring leaders that ever led an army.

The next day the battle of Chancellorsville raged on and although the federals were defeated and were in retreat, there were those who blamed General Colquitt who in his pulling up because of the enemy activity to his right it somehow caused General Jackson to get shot. Although General Colquitt was a hero in the battle of South Mountain, his star had suddenly lost its luster to the Confederate hierarchy. General Hill was first sent to North Carolina and Generals Rhodes and Ramseur took over his command.

Chapter Four: to the Carolinas

On May 20, 1863 Colquitt's brigade was ordered to proceed by rail to Goldsboro, North Carolina and had orders to report to Major General Daniel Harvey Hill, commanding. The brigade gathered up its equipment and boarded the train in Richmond, heading to North Carolina. On May 28th, they arrived in Kinston, North Carolina, where they were encamped. This was the second longest train ride that Willie and Randall had ever taken. They got to look over some of the country they had seen on the way up from Georgia, and somehow, it didn't look the same. This war had been rough on Virginia and North Carolina, and they were sure it'd been rough on their home, Georgia too. On June 22 they were ordered to build a works at Kinston, North Carolina, which they did.

Willie and Randall worked hard on this task with Randall remarking he'd never shoveled so much dirt in his life. They cut down trees and built the breastworks along with the trenches in order to protect the city and the important railroad depot. They were prepared for whatever the enemy would throw at them. They had just completed the building of the works, when orders came for them to head to Wilmington, North Carolina to help check an advance of enemy forces. By July 21, they had arrived at Wilmington and were ordered to Topsail Sound on the next day. They basically performed picket duty until August 10 when they received orders to report to Charleston, South Carolina. On August 13, they arrived in Charleston and marched to James Island where they set up camp. Willie was excited because his father's regiment was still somewhere in the Charleston-Savannah area and he might get a chance to see him.

As they prepared to move out to Charleston, both boys were excited. This would be the closest they had been to home since October 1861, when they had left for Camp Spalding in Griffin.

"You think Charleston will be more like home?" inquired Randall.

"It may be. Although, it's a lot closer to the coast than Appling County is. I bet there are no mountains there. There probably isn't any snow, and it's got to be much warmer. I'm looking forward to being there close to where my father's outfit is, if they're still there. I'm looking forward to seeing him and some of the friends from our old area of the county," responded Willie.

"You reckon we'll be encamped close to them?" inquired Randall.

"I don't know. Word is that we're going to James Island. That's the place that Captain Latimer's company fought early in the war. Mother wrote me about that battle, because some of our kin folks were in it. Obviously, the Yankees didn't win or we wouldn't be setting up camp there," answered Willie.

"I just hope to have plenty to eat. It seems I stay hungry all of the time now," Randall said, as he dug in his haversack for a piece of cornbread to nibble on. Randall always was hungry. The boy could put away some food, if he had it before him.

Their conversation came to an abrupt halt as the sergeant came by and got them all into line. They moved toward a train. After they had loaded all the equipment belonging to the regiment, they grabbed their personal items and scurried aboard the box car. Willie had not even gotten in good, when he felt the jolt of the locomotive starting to pull out.

"You would think that they would at least wait until we all got on. Wonder what the hurry is?" snapped Willie. "I'm sure the war can wait another minute or two."

"Just hold on," said Randall. "Sit down, relax and enjoy the ride."

James Island was a place of encampment for several regiments of Confederate troops. The defense of the coast was of utmost importance to the south. The Yankees lay out beyond the harbor with their gunboats in order to blockade supplies from coming into Charleston Harbor. Blockade runners were popular in the Charleston area. They brought goods in that could not be obtained anywhere else. They were touted for their heroics. All the young ladies of Charleston wanted to keep company with them, for they also had lots of money. Defense of Charleston Harbor consisted of keeping the forts and batteries manned to be able to repel any attack on those positions. Word had spread to the camp that detached companies of the Twenty-seventh would be moving in and out of Fort Sumter to strengthen the garrison there. At times the federal gunboats would shell Fort Sumter in hopes of softening it up. The troops in the garrison would either help to man the cannons or just stay out of harm's way. Company I was to load on the boats, and go spend two weeks there starting next Sunday.

Willie found where the Fifty-fourth Georgia was encamped on James Island but found that his father's company was on Morris Island at a place called Battery Wagner. Morris Island was just across the bay from Fort Sumter, and if someone was in possession of a telescope or field glasses they might be able to see the troops on Morris Island. Willie mused that he might be able to borrow some glasses and maybe even see his father. Willie and Randall had never, ever been on a boat other than real small wooden ones in the edge of the River. This size boat could go very far out and Randall wasn't sure whether he was going to like this or not. This boat was big enough for 100 men. Although he had caught a glimpse of Fort Sumter, he had no idea how far it was and how long it would take to get there. The water in the sound was "white capping" because the wind was blowing so hard. The boat bounced around in the water until Randall started looking queasy.

"What's the matter Randall? You look funny," said Willie.

"I feel funny. I feel like I'm going to upchuck. My stomach is churning," answered Randall.

"You'll be alright Laddie," a voice came from behind them. They turned and looked. It was the captain of the ship. "You just have a touch of seasickness. It's a good thing you're not in the Confederate Navy. You would probably have to spend time on the open sea in a schooner."

"What's a schooner?" Randall asked.

"You see that tall three masted ship over on the port side?" said the captain, as he pointed out the ship with three tall masts and sails all the way up and down them. "That's a schooner, Laddie. We sail the ocean with them."

"I didn't even know what the port side was. I surely don't know what an ocean is," said Randall. "Do you Willie?"

"Nope. But always wanted to see one," answered Willie.

"You'll get to see one soon enough, Laddies. There'll be one right out in front of Sumter for you to look at till ya get tired of seein' it," answered the Captain.

They "saw it a 'plenty" for the next two weeks. Every time they had guard duty and marched up and down on the top of that wall, they could look out to the East and as far as they could see was water. Willie wondered how far it was to France, England and the rest of Europe. He pondered how brave his ancestors had to have been to get on ships like that and sail across an ocean to get to America in the first place.

After two weeks at Fort Sumter, the same boat with the same captain returned to take them back to the mainland.

"Hello Laddies," the captain said as they climbed aboard. "Did you see enough of the Atlantic Ocean while you were there?"

"Yes sir," said Randall snapping to attention. "It would take a long time to drink all that water."

"You could't drank it, Laddie. It's salt water. It'll kill you to drink it," retorted the captain.

"We never got close enough to it to taste it." remarked Randall. "One afternoon though, the sky turned black over the ocean and, the wind started to blow fiercely. Behind that came the worst rainstorm I've ever seen in my life.

"Does it do that when you're crossin' that ocean?" asked Willie.

"It does, Laddie. There are some places like Cape Fear on the North Carolina coast that a many a ship has gone down in those storms there. They call it a graveyard for ships," answered the captain.

"Willie, remind me that I don't want to be in the Navy. I believe I like keeping my feet on the ground or at least in a horse's stirrup with his feet on the ground."

They arrived back in the mainland and as soon as the officers could get the company assembled, they made their way toward James Island. They passed Company A which was to take their place at the Fort. They marched on to James Island and set up camp at their designated place. There they would rest for a while before being sent back out to Fort Sumter.

Randall was boiling up some poached corn after drilling one day. Willie had just brought another armload of wood stores for their cooking needs, when he noticed a familiar figure walking into camp. It was his father. Willie had not seen him since before he and Randall left for Griffin. His dad had already gone to Savannah with the Appling Volunteers. Willie's heart leapt.

"Fancy seeing you boys here," exclaimed his father as he walked up to the fire. "Mind if I have a cup of whatever that is you have in the pot there, Randall."

"You shore can, Mister William," greeted Randall, "if you can stand the taste of it. Willie and I are about to get used to it, although it is a poor substitute for real coffee."

"I know what you mean. We have been living on that same stuff ourselves," said Willie's father. "Willie, looks like you put on a pound or two since I last saw you."

"I have. Not too much fat, mostly muscle. All this drilling, you know. I thought I could walk when I was at home but I never envisioned walking 20 miles a day like we march sometimes. That's carrying all this gear too," remarked Willie. "How have you been Pa?"

"Pretty good, son! We spent time back and forth between Savannah and here. I really like it better here. I believe there are less mosquitoes here in the summer. I never could stand those bitin' devils. I understand you boys been fightn' in Virginia until of late. I've heard a lot about Virginia but never been there. My granddaddy's daddy was from out there on the James River. I expect it got too cold for him up there, and that's why he moved down south," said Willism.

"We've seen the James River," said Randall. "We were even in a few fights there. You know we were in the Seven Days Battle around Richmond. We sent them Yankees scampering back! I guess the country up there is all right in spring and summer and fall but is cold as could be in wintertime. You don't do much fighting in the winter. You mostly try to figure out how to stay warm."

"Willie, I've been hearing from your mama about your exploits up north. It almost killed her when you left. I know you did what you thought you should but you almost broke her heart doin' it. She says you write her regular and I'm glad of that. Shore am glad that I put you through school, so you could learn to write and cipher. I can still remember you settin' by the hearth readin' your schoolbooks, when you were a little feller. You did like to read. I give you that," said William. "Randall, do you ever write your mother?"

"Not much, Mister William," replied Randall. " Writin' comes hard for me, but Willie's been helping me and I'm getting better at it. They furnish us plenty of pencils and paper to write home. I guess they figure we'll stick around longer as long as we know what's going on at home."

"Pa, have many folks in your company gotten sick, shot or died? I know you don't know many of the boys in our company cause they come from the other side of the county, but we've lost several. Some of those I became good friends with. You know we've lost about as many to sickness as we have to the mini ball. Lots of times they call it camp fever, but it sure can get a man down. When they go to the hospital lots of times they don't come back. There are several men of our company buried in that Virginia soil," said Willie.

"Most our boys have been lost to sickness," remarked Willie's dad. " We haven't seen much heavy fighting but expect the Yankees to attack Wagner most anytime. There's nothing they would like better than to be able to silence our guns. We sunk a gunboat last week, whose captain was stupid enough to expose himself for too long, and one of our 32 pounders put a hole in his boat at the waterline. It didn't take him long before all you could see was the mast and them Yankee sailors swimming around trying to avoid being eaten by those sharks that live out there. I'll bet this war has made them fat."

"What's a shark?" asked Willie.

"It's a fish much bigger than those catfish in the Altamaha," replied William, "And it has rows and rows of teeth. I found some of the teeth as we were patrolling the beach one day. I had one big enough to butcher meat better than any knife you've ever seen. It has a little edge on it that would just cut right through flesh. Some of our sailors talk about them following boats, just in case somebody falls off into the water. I've seen them out there swimming around. You know that fin on the top of the catfish? They got a fin like that but lots bigger and when they swim around just that fin sticks out of the water like a sail."

Willie's dad explained it to them to their amazement that something like that lived out in that water. That made both of them less anxious to take that boat ride to Fort Sumter or to join the Confederate Navy.

Extending his hand to Willie and grasping Willie's hand, his father put his other hand on his shoulder and said, "I'm proud of you son, you've made a real man. Your mother would be proud of you, although she's heartbroken that you're gone. Keep writin' her, as that is all she's got until you come home. I better get back to my company before I'm missed. See ya!"

As Willie watched his father walk off into the distance, he had to fight back a tear in his eye. The old man always expected a lot of him and it did his heart good for his father to seemingly approve of how he was turning out and growing up. Willie watched intently as he completely disappeared from sight, and then turned to Randall who said. "I shore would like to see my father and the rest of my family too!"

Sergeant Mann came over presently and inquired as to who the visitor was. Willie told him that it was his father who was in the Fifty-fourth Georgia camped not far away on James Island. He told the sergeant that they had been on Battery Wagner and were rotated out for a few days. Sergeant Mann had become a good friend. He was as brave as anyone Willie had ever known. At Sharpsburg, when all of the hand-to-hand began at the far end of the cornfield, out of the corner his eye, Willie caught sight of Mann fighting them Yankees like an enraged bobcat. Those boys he was tied up with had sure bitten off more than they could chew. He was tearing into them like a house a'fire. Willie would bet he took down some eight or ten of them, before the order to withdraw was given.

"Why did he join that company instead of ours, Willie?" asked the Sergeant.

"I was only 15 when they left. Besides I don't think my father would have let me at the time," said Willie. "It sounded, a while ago, like he might would have let me now."

"Willie, he acted like he might be a little proud of you now," remarked Randall.

"Maybe so," said Willie.

In three days they began to hear the cannon and musketry in the direction of Fort Wagner. It was intense and Willie wondered if his dad was back inside the fort now. The musketry went on for a good long time before it quieted off. Willie's mind was going wide open. He feared for his father's safety. It was different now, than it was when he was in

57

Virginia and his father was here and he didn't know much about what was going on in the Charleston area. Now after visiting with his father it all became real to him concerning the danger that his father could be in. All that musketry over there, with mini balls flying through the air. Some of them could easily be coming into contact with human beings. Willie looked up and saw Major Gardner coming through the camp. Major Gardner was another of those fierce warriors in their company. At Seven Pines he stood firm in the hail of bullets after Captain Lee of their company had gone down and helped to rally the troops. He and Colonel Jenkins of South Carolina had pushed the troops forward and put them in a position where they had broken the center of the Yankee line. They had taken the high ground from them. Willie had a great deal of respect for the man.

Major Gardner had Captain Graham pulled off to the side, and they were discussing something. Willie wished he could hear what they were saying but assumed that he would find out quickly enough. He watched with interest as Captain Graham pulled the other officers and the top sergeants to the side. Presently Sergeant Mann made his rounds in the encampment, informing them they were to quickly cook three days rations and gather up their accouterments, because they were pulling out.

"Where are we going Sergeant?" asked Randall.

"Fort Wagner, that's where it seems the action is. The Yankees attacked there this morning and our boys gave them what for. Word is we didn't suffer many casualties, but the lead element in their attack, the Fifty-fourth Massachusetts, lost about half." Willie had heard of the Fifty-fourth Massachusetts. They were part of the US colored infantry. Loosing half is as much as the Twenty-seventh lost at Sharpsburg. Willie remembered how long it took them to recover and for those who were wounded to get well. He also remembered those he hadn't seen since then. Some of them were taken captive, but lots of them had given their all. Some of that number were his friends. Willie looked around and Randall already had the spider on the coals frying up the bacon. As soon as the bacon was ready, Randall would mix up some cornmeal and make hoecakes for them to pack in their haversacks. Willie began to strike the tent and prepare to move out. It wasn't too long before they were given orders to form up and prepare to move out. They marched to the East through the encampments of some of the other regiments. There were lots of Confederate soldiers on James Island. Many more than Willie had been aware of. They marched until they arrived at their destination where the boats awaited them. They had never considered that Morris Island had a body of water separating it from James Island. They climbed on the boats, crossed the river and formed up on the other side.

They marched until they were inside of Fort Wagner, which was a mostly dirt fort, although the walls were thick log walls with sand piled in their front. When they got there, the dead and wounded from the battle were still being removed and buried. The scene brought back memories to the boys, memories of battles in Virginia and Maryland and the aftermath. They marched right past Fort Wagner and took up a position in front of the Fort on the sandy section of land that he heard someone refer to as a beach. They shucked their accouterments and laid their muskets on top. Shovels were distributed along the line and they began to dig an entrenchment and pile that sand up for protection from shot and shell. In the hot South Carolina weather, Willie quickly removed his sack coat because the wool was getting awfully warm. He laid it on his musket and continued to dig, sweat pouring from his forehead. They were preparing for another attack, which everyone believed was imminent. Their regiment, under Colonel Zachary, was preparing to take the full force of the enemy attack first. They would be the initial point of contact, when the attack occurred. If Willie knew Colonel Zachary, he planned to give them all they wanted and more, if they were foolish enough to take the Twenty-seventh Georgia head-on.

"I ain't never dug so much in my life," stated Randall. "I got pure calluses on my hands."

"The better we dig, the better chance we have of surviving an attack, Randall," said Willy. "I want all the sand I can get between me and them Yankee mini balls, when they start a coming."

"When you reckon they'll come?" Randall inquired, as he threw another shovel full of dirt out in front. "It's been a long time since we were in a good fight. I'm about ready for them to come. We're the only Appling County boys that they haven't met yet. We might get a chance to introduce ourselves in a little while." Randall always could come up with the strangest things at the strangest times, and this was no exception.

"You been in the sun too long Randall. You're talking like a crazy man. Hush up and get back to digging," said Willie.

"Yes sir. Mister Corporal, Sir," replied Randall grinning from ear to ear.

They stayed in that position, without attack, until the sixth of September, when orders were given for them to prepare to be the rear guard as troops were being withdrawn from Fort Wagner. Willie could not understand this because they had held the Yankees off so long, why would they turn around and give them the Fort? Willie's lot was not to question but to follow orders. So he prepared as he was ordered. As they covered the withdrawal some of the men in the regiment were wounded. They had already lost two soldiers, killed by sharpshooters from the union side.

"Watch out, Randall!" snapped Willie as sand flew up between them on the beach. The mini ball had struck too close. Turning around Willie spotted a figure behind a bush about 100 yards from them, on the edge of the woods, taking aim toward them. He quickly raised his musket and squeezed the shot off, watching the blue uniformed soldier roll out onto the beach. He heard another muzzle blast as Randall took a second Yankee in the edge of those same woods.

The withdrawal went smoothly. As they loaded on the boats they were covered by riflemen on the other side of the river. They quickly got across the river, and literally gave Morris Island over to Billy Yank. This left a bad taste in Willie's mouth. He thought they could have held out much longer, but he guessed that's why he wasn't the general and was only a corporal. They had not been on land for very long until they were loaded up and boated to Fort Sumter. From then until February of the next year, 1864, they were shuttled back and forth on detached duty at Fort Sumter.

At one point in time, as Willie and Randall were eating their daily ration, they spotted General Colquitt and another distinguished looking general approaching the headquarters tent. They watched as the two generals met with Colonel Zachary and Major Gardner. The Lieutenant Colonel was in his quarters recovering from what he said was eating a piece of bad meat, so he could not attend the pow-wow. Willie later learned that the other general was General P. G. T. Beauregard. General Beauregard was the one who had fired on Fort Sumter to make the Yankees leave there in the first place after the secession. Everybody knew who General Beauregard was, and Willie could still see the mustache and chin whiskers that he sported even after he had gone. General Beauregard was the commander of the Department of South Carolina, Georgia and Florida. Willie wondered how he would look with a fine set of facial hair like that. He didn't have to worry about it too much, because his beard was not very heavy, and it did not grow very much either. Randall, on the other hand, had dark whiskers and shaved at least once every ten days.

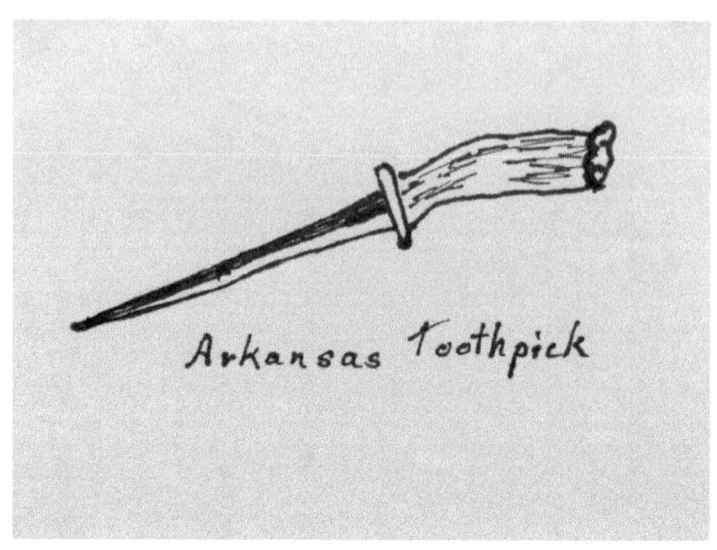

Arkansas Toothpick

Chapter Five: Olustee

By January 23 of 1864 the Twenty-seventh Georgia Regiment was up to the strength of 605 men in the 10 companies. This was the result of some of the wounded returning, the sick getting well and the recruitment effort of the recruitment officers. This regiment, which had started off over 1000 strong, had dwindled in strength mostly due to the losses in battle and those succumbing to illness. On the 8th of February, word spread through the camp that the Regiment was being reassigned. It was reported that they were going to Savannah and were going to report to General Gilmer in Florida. On the 10th of February, they were again on the march. Colonel Zachary was relieved at Fort Johnson. They were again to cook three days rations, which had become the signal that a fight was soon to come. They headed to John's Island, which was on the other side of the Stono River near Secessionville. This was where two battles already occurred. The first, Grimbol's at the Stono, was where Willie had heard that the Appling Rangers of the Forty-Seventh Georgia had suffered some heavy losses at the first of the war. The second was the Battle of Secessionville. They crossed the Stono River on the James Island and marched to join General Wise, who was already engaged with the enemy. They arrived in the nick of time and assisted General Wise in driving the Yankees off the island. Their presence there had made the difference, because as the regiment moved forward into line of battle, the enemy realized they were outnumbered. At this point the enemy decided that discretion was the better part of valor. So they skedaddled!

The Twenty-seventh Georgia turned around and marched back to James Island, just in time to get orders to load up on the Charleston and Savannah railroad. They loaded up on the 14th and took that train to Savannah. Willie and Randall had never seen Savannah and wished that they could stay a while and look it over. They had heard about Savannah all their lives, since it was a bustling port city and was the largest city in their part of the state. Savannah had been there since General Oglethorpe had founded the city for England. That was way before the revolution where Willie's great granddaddy had fought around Charleston with Francis Marion, the "Swamp Fox". His ancestor had even been captured by the British and imprisoned in Charleston for a while. Granddaddy Lewis was a Lieutenant in the North Carolina militia. He ended up in South Georgia due to a bounty land grant which gave him land along the Altamaha River. When the War of 1812 broke out, Lewis and his son-in-law, James were spies West and Southwest of the Altamaha River, scouting movements of the British and the Creek Indians that were their allies.

Savannah was not as large as Richmond but it was surely much larger than Holmesville. They changed trains and got on the Gulf and Atlantic railroad headed west. They crossed the Altamaha River at Doctortown, which really wasn't very far from where Willie and Randall had lived. It was not in Appling County, but it was just down River from Goose Creek, which was the Appling-Wayne County line. At another place called Teabeauville, they again changed trains and continued west. They traveled about fifty miles and the train came to a stop. They unloaded from the cars, formed up and began the march south. They had been told that they were headed toward Lake City, Florida, because a Yankee force was moving in from the East Coast at Cowpens, headed that way. They marched about 20 miles and got on another train, which took them into Lake City. When they arrived at Lake City, they met up with some Florida units, some militia and Colonel Clinch's Fourth Georgia Cavalry. There were boys from Appling County in both Company A and Company I of Clinch's Fourth Georgia Cavalry. Several young men on horses rode by and Randall grabbed Willie by the shoulder and said, "Look! There's Sam Watson! Sam. Sam. What you doing here?"

Turning in his saddle and grinning ear to ear Sam hollered, "Randall, what are you doing here? I thought you and Willie were in Virginia. This is a long ways from Virginia." Sam was mounted on a fine sorrel gelding.

"Man, we've been everywhere. We've been in Maryland, Virginia, North Carolina and we haven't long been left Charleston, South Carolina. Sam we've seen places we'd a never thought we'd a saw in our life," exclaimed Randall. "Old Willie here, has made corporal. He has saved my skin more than one time."

"You two been in many fights?" inquired Sam. "Seen much action?"

To which Willie remarked, "Seen our share of it. It didn't take long before we'd "Seen the Elephant". We were in some big 'ons'. Our job is chasing Yankees."

"Looks like you gonna get to chase them some more. I heard there was a bunch of 'em coming from toward Cowpens while I was on the train at Doctortown." He said stroking his horse's neck. "Old Tom don't like to ride on a train! I even gave him a ration of corn, and he still didn't settle down the whole way here. I was so glad to get off 'at dad burn train, to get back into the saddle that I can't tell ya," said Sam, "I sure am glad I had old Tom here, cause if I didn't, I'd be a foot soldier like you boys. No disrespect you know, but I had never been much on walking, and I hear you boys do a lot of that."

"The only horse we had on the farm had to stay there and pull the plow. We didn't have no extra. But a-walkin' ain't bad, and you get used to it after a while. Sometimes we have marched up to twenty miles in one day," said Willie.

"Twenty miles? I'd die. I told ya I don't like walking at all," retorted Sam. "You fellers shore are tougher than me."

The column of cavalry moved on and the boys wondered if they'd ever see Sam again. His daddy's farm was about five miles from where they lived and they would see them once in a while at a church social. He did like the girls and they seemed to like him too. He did look kind of dashing perched up on that sorrel horse with a revolver on his side and a sword on the other. He had some kind a little short rifle tied off to his saddle. It looked like the muskets that they shot, just a much shorter version. His family always did have a little more money than Willie's and Randall's families did. Both the boys wondered what it would be like to be in the cavalry. Willie still remembered how dashing Captain Mosby was in Virginia, when he saw him that time. One difference though, Mosby didn't carry a saber. As best Willie could recollect he had two revolvers on his waist belt and two more on his saddle in pommel holsters. One of his men had told Randall that the captain would not let his men carry a sword into battle. He said that they made too much racket. He also said that they were only useful for barbecuing a piece of meat over the fire. He wanted his men to carry at least two pistols although he preferred four. If they didn't have four they had to have two extra loaded cylinders so they could swap 'em out quickly. Mosby's Rangers captured enough Yankees that they soon had accumulated enough pistols for everyone to have four. Willie also remembered the feather in Mosby's hat. It was long like a turkey feather but more bushy. Someone had said it was an ostrich plume, but Willie didn't know what an ostrich was, much less what an ostrich plume was. He had also seen that same kind a feather in General Jeb Stuart's hat.

"Randall, you still got that Colt's pistol you took off the Yankee officer?" inquired Willie.

"Yeah, and I got it loaded with .44 caliber balls I got at Fort Sumter from that Lieutenant of Artillery there, the one that I got to know well. He showed me how to load it, and I got some more balls and caps in my haversack along with it. If I just had a horse, I might could jine the cavalry down here. I have to figure out how to get me a sword though," said Randall who had been carrying that pistol around all his time.

66

As far as Willie knew Randall had never even shot that thing. He might not could hit the side of a barn with that thing, thought Willie.

They were given orders to form up and they began to march in an easterly direction. Willie saw General Colquitt up at the head of a column. The Sixth Georgia was directly behind him, and the Twenty-seventh Georgia was next. The territory there around Lake City reminded the boys of home. Pine trees, palmettos and gall berry bushes. They marched until the scouts found the place with a swamp to one side and a great big natural lake to the other that was near to Olustee, the station on the railroad. There was a narrow strip of dry land in between. Willie was no officer but he could tell that would be a good place because the enemy couldn't flank you there. They would have to take you head on. That would be to the enemy's disadvantage, because the boys in Colquitt's Brigade knew how to shoot. The general positioned the artillery batteries so that they could cover the field. The general that was really in charge, who was from Florida, had never led men in battle, so he deferred to General Colquitt, the "Rock of South Mountain." Skirmishers were sent out with the intention of engaging the enemy and drawing them into the place of General Colquitt's choosing.

Initially in the battle, the Twenty-seventh Georgia and the Sixth Georgia, the two best regiments in the brigade were placed in the reserve. The battle worked out just as General Colquitt wanted it. The enemy was drawn in by the skirmishers and then by the cavalry, right into the teeth of Colquitt's main line of defense. The battle raged for a while and it was hard to tell who was winning, because the Yankees outnumbered the Confederates, but not nearly as bad as the brigade had seen in the past. Someone later said there were 5200 confederates and 5500 federals.

As the tide of battle was switching back and forth, the Confederates on the frontline had almost exhausted all 60 rounds of ammunition they had in their cartridge pouches. The men were given orders to hold their position, even though they were mostly out of ammunition. The other three regiments of Colquitt's brigade who were experienced held well, but even the militia held; just when you thought that it was about to give way, General Colquitt's brother, Lieutenant Colquitt, grabbed up the Georgia flag and stuck it in his stirrup and rode up and down that line to encourage everybody. Those troops in the front let out a "Rebel Yell" that probably made those Yankees blood run cold. Someone had taken a carriage and gathered up the ammunition from the dead and wounded and brought it to the front lines for distribution amongst the troops. At the same time, the Sixth and Twenty-seventh Georgia regiments were ordered up into line. Colonel Zachary was in the lead of the regiment, and with a raised sword, he led them in. As they fired a volley, with fixed bayonets, they charged headlong into the enemy. The Twenty-seventh never stopped nor slowed down. They started the rout and the Yankees left in such a hurry that they left their dead, wounded and several field pieces there on the battlefield. The Yankees skedaddled back toward Cowpens and the Atlantic Ocean with the Twenty-seventh and the Sixth Georgia in hot pursuit. The Twenty-seventh had gone through the troops in their front like a hot knife through butter. They later found that some of these were the Fifty-fourth Massachusetts, the colored troops that had suffered so many losses at Battery Wagner. Willie's estimate was that they may have lost half their number there at Olustee.

Two days later, at Cedar Creek, under the command of Colonel Zachary, the Confederate forces almost caught the rest of the Yankees. It was said that Colonel Zachary reported that if Colonel Clinch had closed the gate, they would have caught them all. The Yankees would have either fought to the death or been captured and sent to Andersonville along with the rest of the prisoners. The Yankees then retreated all the way to the East Coast and put their backs to the Atlantic Ocean. Their attempt to cut the railroad that led out of Lake City and stop the transport of Florida beef to feed the Confederacy failed miserably.

Willie was placed in charge of caring for the wounded. Among them was Randall who had a flesh wound in his left arm. It looked bad, and he was lucky that it didn't hit the bone. Willie was sure that Randall would heal. He was tough. They also learned that Sam had caught a mini ball in the chest and expired there on the battlefield. Willie wondered if old Tom had gone down too with his friend. Lots of times the horses, being bigger targets were more apt to be hit than their riders. Willie was feeling melancholy about losing another friend. Their company had one killed, private John Cooner. There were six or seven out of the company wounded, including one of Willie's good friends Ben and Sergeant Mann. Willie and Randall had met Ben when they were in Camp Stephens at Griffin. Willie took an immediate liking to him, because he was a bubbly energetic and funny boy. He was only about a year older than Willie but sometimes acted younger. They were at Camp Milton while they were trying to recover after the battle. They stayed there about a month recuperating. Willie was in charge of a detail of five soldiers who were tasked with looking out for those wounded soldiers.

They were informed that the federal troops had lost almost half, 2600 killed, wounded and captured. The Confederate forces had less than 1000 in that same category. On April 16, 1864, General Colquitt was ordered to move the Twenty-seventh back to the Georgia coast. They marched to Callahan, Florida. Then they marched to Traders Hill and then to Teabeauville, where they were to board the train for Savannah. As they marched into Teabeauville they were greeted by a small group of people who cheered as they marched past. As they neared the train station, the First Sergeant called the troops to a halt and after giving them some instructions, dismissed the Regiment. Some with minor wounds like Randall were on the march with the Regiment, while others more seriously wounded had been left in Camp Milton.

Willie walked over to Randall and inquired how his arm was healing to which Randall replied, "It is tolerable, although is still burns a mite."

"Be sure to keep it clean," Willie instructed Randall. Although Willie was not a surgeon, he in other battles and over the last few days he had spent a lot of time with the surgeon and was well-versed in taking care of gunshot wounds. "You need to get a clean bandage on that thing before it gets infected."

"Oh! Boys can we help you? " a girl's voice from behind Willie said.

Looking around, Willie saw two of the prettiest girls he had ever seen. One was a blonde who was tall and slim, and the other was a brunette who was a little shorter. "Would you know where we might can find some clean bandages fur old Randall here, would you?" Willie inquired not being able to take his eyes off the pretty blonde. She smiled and her pretty blue eyes sparkled as she answered, "Sure we have some, Mary, change the bandage on that poor boy's arm."

Randall blushed as the cute brunette removed the old bloody, dirty bandage and began to tenderly wrap his arm with a new, clean piece of cotton cloth. "T-T-T-Thank you kindly ma'am," he stammered. The thought of this pretty girl giving him attention like that was unsettling. Randall had always been a little shy around girls, and this was really getting to him. His face turned red, as if he'd been working in the hot sun all day long.

"What is your name ma'am?" Willie inquired of the pretty blonde.

"Sally. Sally Smith." she answered. "Pleased to make your acquaintance." She was smiling and blinking those pretty blue-eyes at him. Willie felt something funny in his chest like his heart was fluttering. This was without a doubt the prettiest girl he had ever seen, and she was actually talking to him.

"You from around here, Sally?" Willie inquired.

She pointed over behind her to a whitewashed house. "I live right there by the railroad track," she answered. "Mary lives two houses down."

They spent the rest of the afternoon talking with the two girls. Willie was not sure just how far it was from his home in Appling County to Teabeauville, but he was sure that that railroad track ran from Doctortown, which is only about 10 miles from his family farm to there. He was also sure he could find the way back. He would remember what that house looked like.

70

The peace and tranquility of the visit was shattered when he heard the first Sergeant's voice booming, "Fall in men. In line by files. March." They did as they were ordered and marched toward the open cars on the train which looked to be headed East. Willie and Randall took one look back around at the two girls they had met and wondered if they would ever see them again.

Within three days they were back on James Island and had set up camp in the very place they left about a month and a half ago. Within a couple of days, they were all sent to Fort Sumter and were garrisoned there. They stayed in Fort Sumter until they received orders to return to Virginia.

stiching up
the leg.

Chapter Six: Back to Virginia

By May 12, the regiment, along with the brigade, was in Petersburg, Virginia. They just got there in time to engage the US Calvary in a skirmish near Petersburg. They were quickly moved to Weldon railroad in anticipation of an attack there. The attack did not come, but by May 16, they were at Drewry's Bluff, Virginia, at Fort Darling. Randall was all healed up by now and would roll his sleeve up and show everybody his scar. He had remembered that Mary had said that they ought to give a medal to you just for being wounded, but Willie told her that was silly, for it would be a waste of metal to make a medal for him. General Colquitt became the division commander and Colonel Zachary was the brigade commander and Lieutenant Colonel Gardner took command of the Twenty-seventh Georgia. They were engaged in a battle with nearly 40,000 union troops. Although the Twenty-seventh Georgia was initially put in the reserve, they were brought up quickly at Swift Creek to support General Ransom's division and then moved to support

General Hoke as he drove the federal force back. The Twenty-seventh Georgia took several casualties along with the remainder of the brigade.

After the battle, the boys were resting trying to catch their breath when the sergeant came by." You boys doin' all right? Neither of you got hit? We've come through another one hadn't we?"

"Yes sergeant. We came out all right. Just how many Yankees are there in this world? We just keep shooting and killing 'em, and they keep coming," Randall inquired.

"Why Randall, you first got to understand they have twice as many states as the Confederacy does, and in those states they don't do much farmin' and have bigger cities. So I guess they must have five or six times as many people as we do. That means that they would have to have five or six times as many soldiers as we do."

"But I done kilt way more than my five," said Randall "And they are still a coming."

"I reckon our regiment has all killed way more than their five. Somebody's not holding up their end of the work or we'd be through by now."

"I guess as long as they keep 'a-comin' we'll keep a shootin!" said Willie. "Maybe they're at least through a-comin' for today anyway."

The Confederate army had dug trenches and built breastworks all around the city of Petersburg. Some had referred to General Robert E. Lee as the King of Spades, because of all the shovel work they had done. Warfare had changed from the tactics of Napoleon where two armies would just clash up close on the field of battle.

The greatest reason for the change was that where Napoleon's troops shot smoothbore muskets that were accurate up to about 60 yards. The modern army was shooting muskets with range that is ten times that much. Some sharpshooters shot Whitworth rifles that were accurate up to 1000 yards. Randall was telling Willie one day about the general that was scolding the union troops under him, because they were trying to stay undercover with the sharpshooters of the Confederacy firing at them. The general was said to have told them, "Don't be afraid of them Rebs, boys. They couldn't hit an elephant from there." Suddenly a ball from a Confederate sharpshooter's rifle struck him between the eyes knocking him from his horse. He was dead before he hit the ground. The Yankee troops were even more afraid of the Confederate sharpshooters after that.

Around Petersburg there were lots of potshots taken by sharpshooters from both sides. A soldier quickly learned to keep his head down and not present a target that was easily hit. The pickets had to be awfully careful too because the sharpshooters took no mercy on them. There was skirmishing sometimes day and night at those positions around Petersburg but before the month was over they were moved to a place that they were all too much familiar with. Cold Harbor, Virginia was the place. They remembered it from 1862 in the Seven Days Battle around Richmond. The Regiment had suffered heavy casualties in that battle in '62. Willie remembered especially because he had lost several friends. Here they were again.

Sergeant Mann, who was leading this action, had been wounded both at Cold Harbor and at Olustee, was telling them earlier that he never did like this place. He still could remember the pain of the wound in his arm. They were in position on the evening of May 30 at that place with pickets in advance of the regiment. The pickets found the enemy works and withdrew back to the lines. This was where we commenced to build works of our own. General Lee supervised the construction of the works, himself. He had them built so if the Confederates were able to draw the enemy in where they wanted them, they would be able to enfilade their flanks.

The Sixth Georgia and the Twenty-seventh Georgia were again on the right and in position to enfilade the enemy, if the opportunity presented itself. Willie and Randall again were side-by-side as they prepared for the upcoming battle. Willie began to think about 1862. He mused about the fact that the Seven Days Battle came on the heels of the Seven Pines Battle. He remembered the destruction and devastation that happened in those seven days. He remembered the carnage and the casualties of those battles. Was it about to begin again? Would there be another Seven Days Battle around Richmond?

The Yankees had a new general, General Ulysses S. Grant. This was about the fifth general that President Lincoln had chosen to lead the invading northern army. The boys wondered if it would be some more of the same. Their goal was to make Mister Lincoln have to choose another one because of failure. On the morning of June 1, all questions would be answered. The attack began early. It was a brisk skirmishing to the left of the Regiment, and then they were involved quickly thereafter. The Yankees would charge into the place that General Lee thought they would, and the Confederate musketry would deal death and carnage to them. They charged again with the same result. They just kept coming. And they just kept falling. Willie heard a thump to his right and saw Sergeant Mann go down. He heard a yelp from Randall as a bullet grazed his ear.

"Keep your head down, Randall!" shouted Willie, "If you don't, they will shoot it off your shoulders."

"I will, Willie, Them rascals have done and went and got my ear," replied Randall.

Willie looked over at his friend and saw blood streaming down his ear and onto his shoulder. That was close. Too close! Willie could have lost his best friend just that quickly. The Yankees kept coming and they kept falling. Willie later learned that General Grant would be referred to as the "Butcher", because he would keep sending his troops in unlike the generals before him, who would take a licking and then back up. This might be another kind of enemy to face. He didn't know when he was whupped. The regiment stayed there and fought for several days. There was no telling how many Yankees went down in their front.

Again, Willie had exhausted his 60 rounds of cartridges and had to be replenished by the quartermasters. Randall had almost emptied his cartridge pouch too, so he replenished it. Grant sent them Yankees in and General Lee's boys were stacking them up like cordwood in their front. At one time Willie's barrel had gotten so hot that he couldn't even touch it. Nevertheless, he kept firing and firing, and the Yankees kept coming and coming.

The regiment itself had suffered several casualties including Sergeant Livingston, who was shot dead. They held that position until the 13th of June when they marched toward the enemy and another familiar place, Malvern Hill. Randall had finally gotten his ear to stop bleeding and looked much better than he did with blood streaming down the side of his head and onto his neck and collar. Sergeant Mann had been evacuated to the receiving hospital, and they guessed on the road to Chimborazo hospital after that. Finally, all the hostilities were about to come to a cease. They had passed through Seven Pines, which also brought back bad memories of the campaign of 1862. They had a small fight on Malvern Hill, but unlike the first occasion they quickly drove the federals off the hill in today's fight. They had taken the railroad back to Petersburg and were again on the Petersburg line.

Captain Graham came by where Willie and Randall were stationed and talked with them a bit. He informed Willie that he was now Sergeant and Randall that he was now a Corporal. Randall was beside himself for he never thought he'd be anything more than a private. Willie told him not to let the rank go to his head, because with that rank came more responsibility. Both boys were proud that they had been recognized as being good soldiers. They were proud also that they were still alive and that the only thing that had happened to Randall was his ear had gotten nicked. Willie wondered what his father would've thought of him now being a Sergeant, because he seemed proud that he was a Corporal back in Charleston. He wondered about his father and where he might be. He had a letter from his mother saying that they had been moved from the Georgia coast after the battle of Chickamauga. They had been sent to Dalton to join the Army of Tennessee. They were engaged with an army led by General Sherman who by all accounts was a ruthless commander who believed in flanking to gain an advantage. Willie had hoped that his father would fare well in the battles that awaited him. He longed for another reunion with him but didn't know when that might occur. They might as well be two worlds apart. His mother had also said in the letter that Lizzie, who was 15 years old now, had a boyfriend. Willie thought he might like to have talked with that boy about how his sister needed to be treated, but he wouldn't be able to do that until this war was over and they were able to go back home. Randall had gotten a letter too. Although his mama didn't write well, she had gotten the preacher to write a letter to him for her. Randall had already read that letter only three times since he got it. He missed his family as much as Willie missed his. In all this correspondence Randall had greatly improved in his reading and writing skills, which were a requirement for a noncommissioned officer in the army.

On June 16, 1864, the Yankees had come out of Fort Stedman and taken the high ground that the Confederates were holding. They had charged so hard that Haygood's Brigade had just completely given up the position of advantage. They also had a big mortar over there somewhere to the left of that position that would make the loudest boom when it shot. Willie was sure it would wreak devastation wherever it landed.

The Twenty-seventh was ordered forward under Lieutenant Colonel Gardiner. With some fierce fighting they took the position back and ran the Yankees back to Fort Stedman. The Yankees came back five or six times, but each time were turned away. Willie and Randall's muskets got so hot from firing that you could hardly touch the barrel without burning their hand. They learned to pour water down the barrel to cool it off. They held that position for five days without any reinforcements. They turned the Yankees back at least a dozen times in five days, but they did not move and held their ground. That piece of ground later became known as "Colquitt's Salient" for Colquitt held that piece of ground for the remainder of the siege against Petersburg. Willie and Randall had to keep their heads down, because Yankee sharpshooters would rather shoot sergeants and corporals than privates. The Twenty-seventh held the high ground and had sharpshooters of their own. They would "epaulette hunt". That meant that they would wait for an officer to expose himself and then try to take him out of the action. Sharpshooters didn't want to be identified as one if he was captured because the other side hated the sharpshooters and what they did. Willie had been offered the chance to be a sharpshooter because of how well he shot, but he really was not interested.

On several occasions Willie and Randall had hunkered down in the trench and when they saw Yankees scrambling around in the trees, would take the opportunity to pop one. They had put several Yankees out of commission that way. The fighting of the evening of June 18 was fierce, leaving many wounded and several killed in all of the action. Lieutenant Colonel James B. Gardner, one of the bravest soldiers Willie had ever seen, was wounded at the salient during one of those assaults. He died a few days later due to his wound. He was missed by the complete Regiment for he had been in their front on all the actions from Seven Pines until the present.

The Appling Grays had two killed and two more wounded which included Randall's acquaintance, Joseph. Joseph would come over and sit with the two drinking Randall's brew of parched corn. Willie was lucky to be Randall's mess mate because the boy could cook, and he could boil up that bitter brew that would warm all the way to your toes on a cold winter night. Every once in a while, they would shoot a squirrel and Randall would make squirrel stew if he had a potato or some kind a root to put in there. The trick to shooting a squirrel is that you had to make sure you did a good job of head shooting him because that .58 caliber mini ball would totally destroy the squirrel, if you hit them in the body. Randall could make that thing taste really well, and if he had just a little bit of salt to put in it, it was as good as anyone's stew. The broth was just so soothing to drink it down. If they got a squirrel or rabbit they usually would have company unless they kept it a secret.

They had made some friends of several soldiers in Company B which was from up around Macon, Georgia. One of them, John Wesley Bowers was a Corporal like Randall and was a really nice fellow. He had told Willie and Randall that his father had bought a land lot in Appling County for $35 in the early 1840s and had held onto it for three or four years. He then sold it for $50 for a $15 profit. That was for a 490 acre land lot, which Willie quickly ciphered was a whopping $.10 an acre. That was unheard of. Willie and Randall had talked about when they returned after the war trying to find some land and purchase it and farm it together. They could neither imagine owning a tract of land of 490 acres. They were sure they'd still have to help at home around the farm but it would be nice to grow some of their own crops and be able to sell them. Willie had hoped that one day he would be able to have a "riding horse" like old Tom, and Randall had also been wanting a "riding horse" for a long time. He wanted one like Sam had at Olustee. At 19 years old, they really didn't have high goals set for themselves beyond survival of this war. That was going to be a trick itself. With all those Yankee balls flying all over the place, Randall had caught three already, although they didn't hurt much. Willie had gone through unscathed. He supposed the Lord must be looking out for him, because he had not yet taken a hit.

While on duty, a boy from Company G came over one night to where Willie and Randall were holding their post down. The way they worked it was that one would sleep and one would watch. When you stayed in the trenches for a good long time a body would learn to make a little shelter to stay out of the sun when not involved in shooting or ducking. This boy's name was Elias from across the river in Tattnall County, and he lived probably not 5 miles as the crow flies from Willie and Randall. Elias slid under their shelter, reached into his sack coat and pulled out a little bottle.

"What's that in the bottle?" inquired Randall as Elias took a sip.

"It's a little corn liquor," came the reply.

"Where did you get it?" asked the ever curious Randall.

"Got it at a sutler's wagon the other day. You want a sip?" asked Elias.

"No, never touch the stuff. Anyway, it makes some folks crazy," Randall stated.

"Not me!" exclaimed Elias.

"It did my Uncle Jim," stated Randall, "And I don't want to act like an idiot like he did."

"I remember your Uncle Jim," piped Willie. "He sure was a hoot when he got into them squeezins'."

"Momma would take the broom and run him out of the house if he came around, while partaking of that bad stuff," stated Randall with a firm resolve.

Elias took the hint and moved on down the trench to pester someone else more sociable than Randall. The two sat there and discussed the evils of alcoholic drinks. Neither had ever tried it, not even once.

The Twenty-seventh Georgians had to remain on the alert day and night, for the Yankees were apt to attack anytime. There was an attack, late in the evening, on their right, on June the 30th, resulting in the Yankees losing several killed and captured. Private Dunn of Company A told Randall that the Yankees had better sense than to charge our works. Every time they did we would whip them again. The Twenty-seventh Regiment moved in and out of the salient as they were replaced by other regiments. On July 6th, they were relieved by Martin's Brigade, which was at the time under the command of Colonel Charles T. Zachary. It seems like every time a brigade commander goes down, they'll call Colonel Zachary to command the brigade.

At the crack of day on the 30th July, as Randall was boiling some more of that fake coffee he made and was cooking up some bacon, when they were jolted by this tremendous explosion off to their right. Willie rose up to look see what was going on. He saw this cloud of smoke and dirt in the air. They wondered what that could be. They'd never heard a cannon sound that loud. Then all hell broke loose. Yankees over there were shooting cannons. They were firing the artillery and when the smoke cleared that day, the Yankee loss was 3500 men to the Confederate lost around 800 to 1000. The next day word reached their line that the Yankees had tunneled up under the Confederate breastworks and planted explosives. When they set them off, it blew a great crater in the earth. The Yankees tried to breach the line by going in, but they had blown such a deep hole the Confederates who were stationed there made a remark that it was like shooting fish in a barrel. They could not get away from them and their muskets. That was the most unusual thing that Willie and Randall could've ever imagined. They found out later that those Yankees were miners from somewhere up north and thought they could break the line with that little trick. They found out differently.

Colquitt's Brigade fought hard to keep that real estate they had won with so much blood. For the next several days they were rotated in and out of the salient. They would sleep in the trenches when they were at the salient and would sleep in their tents when they were pulled back to the encampment. They would remain assigned to the area near Colquitt's Salient until August 17, when Martin's Brigade relieved Colquitt's Brigade at the salient.

They marched southward, reaching the Weldon and Petersburg railroad. They spent the night there and were initially in the reserve as the Confederate and union troops clashed. Just after midday the Twenty-seventh Regiment was ordered forward. They engaged the enemy with a furious attack. They raised the rebel yell and crashed into the blue line, which quickly gave. They began to push the Yankees back. They began rolling the Yankee line up with a flanking maneuver. As they moved forward, Willie noticed that Company B had captured a stand of enemy colors, and it looked like they had a general officer too. They let out another rebel yell and continued forward. They actually had overextended themselves and got flanked also. This allowed the general to escape and caused several in Company B to be captured. One of them was Corporal John Wesley Bowers, who had become a good friend to Willie over the last two years. As they withdrew from the position and began to retrace some of the ground over which they had charged. Willie and Randall grabbed the fallen comrade, Bluford Sapp, of their company. They drug him back into the protection of their formation. Bluford was wounded in the chest, and blood was gushing from the wound. Willie recognized that his old buddy most likely would not make it even in Jackson Hospital. After trying to comfort Blue he saw him take his last breath. This was the same brave and heroic soldier who had dragged Sergeant Ben Millikin over by the tree at Sharpsburg after he had been wounded in the leg. Blue was the only casualty of Company I that day.

The next day Colquitt's Brigade relieved Ransom's Brigade on the Petersburg line. The siege of Petersburg was continuing as the Yankees looked for soft spots in the line to attack. In late September they were moved to a position over near Fort Harrison. They began to build earthworks and breastworks which would be called Fort Colquitt. On September 29, they were attacked by General Ord's federal troops. The brigade held the union troops at bay for three days at that position. They were then moved back onto the Petersburg line, where for the next two weeks the same scenario occurred over and over again. The Yankees would attack. The Confederates would drive them back. It seemed that Grant did not mind how many men he lost. Willie surmised that it might be because he had so many more than Marse Robert had. They were now in Hoke's Division and got word that they were going to be moved back to North Carolina. Their Christmas present that year was going to be spending Christmas at Greensboro, North Carolina. After several moves, including one to Raleigh, they rejoined the rest of Colquitt's brigade at Wilmington, North Carolina, where they set up camp.

"Randall, I guess it's a little warmer here than it would be up around Petersburg isn't it?" said Willie as they sat around the fire trying to stay warm. Randall had actually traded for some of Mister Lincoln's coffee and they were enjoying and savoring every sip.

"Yeah," replied Randall. "I wonder what the weather's like in Teabeauville."

"Probably a lot warmer than it is here," remarked Willie, as he thought of that long blonde hair and pretty blue eyes of Sally's. Willie wondered if he and Randall would survive this war. He knew that they had been close several times to not doing so. But their task was to follow orders, go where the commanders sent them and to fight like the devil until those blue bellies went back across the Potomac River to stay.

wooden canteen

Chapter Seven: North Carolina Again

It was January 1, 1865 and in order to eat they had to forage for food. "I'll bet that we have walked 10 miles today foraging, and all I have is two skimpy ears a corn and this ole piece of salt pork the lady gave us in that house about 30 minutes ago. The Yankees will not have to kill me I believe I'm going to starve to death," remarked Randall.

A day or two earlier Willie had cut a spear from a sapling and had snared two bass which they had roasted over the fire. It felt like their younger days on the Altamaha River, when they would do that in the oxbow lakes which were the old river runs. They were also good at "Striking", which was using a club while holding a lit lightered knot for a light. Food was important in the winter of 1864 – 1865. Provisions were not as abundant as they had been when they first enlisted. The boys were bound and determined to last this thing out. Although the future did not look as bright as it did at first. No matter how many "Yankees" they killed, they just kept a comin'.

General Colquitt had received orders to take over command of Fort Fisher, a vital fort on the outer banks. The Regiment again took up a line of march. They were on the narrow strip of land nearing the fort when they discovered that federal troops blocked the bridge leading to the fort. The Yankees had landed and had the fort surrounded in an attempt to force it's surrender. Monitor boats were on each side of the strip of land. The Yankees tried for three hours to take the fort but were unsuccessful. The attempt was continued for the next two days. The monitors were shelling the Twenty-seventh Georgia's position. Willie was told that Colonel Lofton of the Sixth Georgia had been killed by a shell, and that General Hoke had climbed a tree to get a better view of the field and had been wounded while in the tree.

"What was he doing up a tree?" Randall asked. "He's too old to be a'climbing trees."

"That sounds like something that we would do," remarked Willie, thinking of all the trees he had climbed in and around the river swamp. He longed to see home again. He and Randall had not been able to get a furlough to go home. Some in his unit had been wounded bad enough to take a furlough home, and others had escorted bodies of their friends and fellow soldiers back home. It had been almost three and a half years since they had seen Appling County, although in February and March of 1864 they had twice passed within a mile of the county line as the train passed through Doctortown in Wayne County. This was before and after the Battle of Olustee.

Fort Fisher was surrendered and General Colquitt had escaped capture. The Twenty-seventh was again the rear guard as they withdrew back toward Wilmington. One of the officers had said that "Old Zach", that is Colonel Zachry, loved to be the rear guard so he could make the enemy pay dearly for the real estate he got. They fought their way back across the narrow strip of land with monitors firing from both sides of them, but pay, the enemy did. Willie saw many of the blue coats fall in the action while the confederates lost many less. By the last of January they were back at Sugar Loaf, North Carolina and were again encamped. The Yankees were continually harassing and trying to get an advantage.

Willie and Randall had picket duty on more than one occasion. One night, Randall detected movement and yelled out "Halt! Who is there?" His answer was musket fire. He and Willie took cover, as the Yankees fired in the dark. The mini balls weren't even coming close. They just hunkered down and waited them out. They were firing blindly in their direction. Randall spotted one of them. He raised his Springfield to his shoulder and squeezed the trigger. The smoke from his musket obscured his view, but Willie told him that he had hit his mark. The Yankee fell with a moan. Suddenly, musket fire rang out all along the picket line, and the Yankees quickly retreated into the safety of the darkness. The trouble with being on picket was that you could have no fire by which to warm. The North Carolina nights were cold in early February.

Everyone knew after the fall of Fort Fisher, that it would not be long before Wilmington came under attack. The pickets had been dealing with the Yankees ever since their return from Fort Fisher, and the buildup of men in blue had not gone without notice of the southern boys. Wilmington came under attack and the men fought hard to defend the city. But when they made the decision to evacuate the Twenty-seventh Georgia, led by "Old Zach", was again the rear guard. They gave up the ground grudgingly and again caused those Yankees to pay dearly for that real estate. Several of the members of the Twenty-seventh were captured as they withdrew. The Regiment moved all the way back to Schofield, North Carolina. They were again engaged on March 8 at Kinston, North Carolina. The fighting was bitter and several times the enemy was turned back. Again, the Regiment lost troops who were captured. They were down to a mere shadow of what they had been when first organized in Griffin in the summer of 1861. There's fighting still to be done and none of them would shirk away from it. On March the 10th, Colquitt's brigade and Kirkland's brigade executed a flanking movement against the union forces and carried the breastworks. Turned out they took most of the troops as prisoners and also captured their artillery pieces. Willie and Randall had taken one artillery piece which was a Parrot gun.

Randall asked Willie, "Reckon we could learn how to shoot this thing? It sure is big and shiny and they have lots of powder and shot for it."

"I'm sure we could," answered Willie. "We've learned how to do a lot of things in the last three and half years. I'm sure we could become artillery men too, if necessary."

"I bet them Yankees know now that the Twenty-seventh ain't got give up, in it!" proudly remarked Randall. "I wonder how many Yankees we've killed now, Willie?"

Willie pondered for a moment and then answered, "Quite a few I would guess. And I bet we got several more in us 'fore they finally take us down. If I get kilt tomorrow, that Yankee army will know that I have been here in their front. They'll know that Willie and Randall from South Georgia have fought hard against them and had sent several of them to an early grave."

"And gonna send several more before it's over!" retorted Randall as he looked over their prize. "Old Zach would be proud to see this piece in our line instead of theirs."

The next day the Regiment again took up a line of march toward the city of Goldsboro. Their brigade which began over 5000 strong had now dwindled to a little over 1000 in number. On March 18th, at a little town named Bentonville, North Carolina, they faced the full force of General Sherman's Army. They had been joined by the Army of Tennessee, who had suffered severe losses at Franklin, Tennessee, not too very long ago. Now the Army of Tennessee and the Army of Georgia, South Carolina and North Carolina were combined.

They not only faced the troops they had fought around Fort Fisher, but now they faced Sherman's Horde. They had heard what Sherman had done to Georgia and South Carolina and were both worried about their dear Appling County and their friends and family there. Had he gone through there and burned and looted like he did in the other places his army had pillaged through. The only salvation for the county was that

Sherman came through there in midwinter. Usually during that time, the Altamaha would be on a fresh. The water would probably be wiregrass to wiregrass which means close to Willie and Randall's homes it would be about 3 miles wide and rushing toward the Atlantic Ocean at a pretty good clip. Unless the enemy would be able to get across somewhere on one of the ferries, they would be very foolish to try to swim that big muddy torrent, and a horse wouldn't have a prayer.

Willie had not received a letter from home since before leaving Petersburg. He guessed the mail might catch up with him one day. He longed to hear his mother's voice. He wondered the fate of his father who was somewhere down the line to his right, and if he had survived Franklin. There was no time to visit, only time to prepare one more time to meet the enemy on the field of battle. He looked across the lines and wondered what his fate would be that day.

"Willie, there sure are a lot of them over there. Reckon how many there are?" said Randall as they stood in line side-by-side one more time.

"All of Sherman's Army and that bunch that we fought at Fort Fisher and Wilmington. They are quite a few there," stated Willie.

"I wonder how many of these battles more we are going to have to fight in before it's over?" said Randall.

"I guess we'll fight till we whup 'em or they whup us!" said Willie as he checked his equipment to make sure everything was in order. His musket was loaded. He had 60 paper cartridges in his cartridge pouch. His cap pouch full. His bayonet was sharp. He guessed he was ready, or at least he hoped so. Thoughts ran through his head of home and of his family and friends. He thought of Sally with her blue eyes and long blonde hair. He would not be killed this day. He had too much to live for. And he would do all he could to make sure Randall made it through this too. They had been through too much together.

89

First Sergeant Mann came down the lines to help in the preparation of the company. Captain Graham had become major for the regiment and there really weren't enough in the company to warrant a command of their own. "Old Zach" had been moved down to command another brigade. In that brigade, there were cadets from one of the North Carolina military schools. Some of them didn't look like they were over 12 or 13 years old, but they looked like they had grit and were ready to fight. Old Zach was just the kind of leader that could get the best out of them.

Randall said, "My Springfield is cleaned, oiled, loaded and ready for action, Willie!"

"Mine too, Randall," answered Willie "We ain't never faced old Billy Sherman before. I hear he likes to flank. They'll be no flanking today, 'cause we are strung out for a long ways in either direction. He'll have to take us head on today. We'll show them what South Georgia River Boys can do."

yonKee canteen

Chapter Eight: The Last Battle

Willie caught a glimpse of General Hoke, General Colquitt and General Johnston mounted on their horses and having a conversation. Willie greatly admired those generals, who had led him through this war. He had the utmost respect, especially for General Colquitt, who on one occasion had stopped and talked with him and Randall, while they were on picket duty. The general seemed like a regular guy to him, but he didn't earn the nicknames "the Rock of South Mountain' and the "Hero of Olustee" without being a bold leader, and how he directed his men in battle, and put the enemy on the run with his tactics.

"Willie, what you think they're talking about back there? Are they going to send us in first? When do you think we're going to start?" Randall was always nervous before a battle, and this was the 44th time that they would be in pitched battle. Randall's nervousness was what Willie believed made him such a good soldier. When he got cranked up, the Yankees had better watch out. Randall could fight with ferocity, and had on several occasions, with bayonet fixed, charged into the enemy like a wild sow defending her piglets. Although, they only had one shot in that

Springfield without reloading, the bayonet and the butt of the stock were both tools of war. Willie remembered when Randall plunged headlong at Olustee, and personally took one artillery piece as the Yankees began to skedaddle, when the Twenty-seventh came into the battle. Randall was Willie's best friend and one of the bravest fighters he had ever seen to not yet be 20 years of age.

"We'll know soon, Randall. 'cause there comes General Colquitt to confer with the rest of the officers of the brigade and I'm sure we'll soon be in action," said Willie as he checked one more time his accouterments, his cartridge pouch and his cap pouch to ensure that he had the full 60 cartridges in there, because he was sure he would need every one of them on this day. There were more Yankees in their front than he had seen since Sharpsburg. He could look across the way and see the bayonet's gleaming in the sun. Fear was not in his makeup for he had seen "the elephant" a long time ago. He began to work himself up for the upcoming action. He reached in his haversack and pulled a piece of dried meat from it that he had been saving back. He quickly ate it and lifted his canteen to his lips to take a swig of cool water. He was ready!

First Sergeant Mann came down the line again. He pointed across the way to a breastwork that had three trees standing tall behind it. He said, "Boys, we are to direct our attack toward the breastworks where those three trees stand. General Colquitt has said it looks weaker there than any other place in our front, so we are to concentrate our efforts, and try to break the line there. If we hit them Yankees hard enough, they'll give way."

Willie looked to his right and there was his old buddy, Joseph Crapps. He remembered how Joseph liked to be on picket duty, because he carried a big Bowie knife and loved to slip over at night to see if he could take out some of the Yankee pickets. Willie knew one thing for sure, he would've hated to be one of those Yankees, if Joseph got a hold of him. He was thin and wiry but strong as an ox. He was also brave as a panther on the prowl. Willie always thought Joseph might be a little bit crazy and had a pretty bad temper. You did not cross him.

"Randall, I bet I beat you to those trees today."

"Willie, you never could out run me, and I don't intend to stop until I get there. When I do, I'll look around and see how far behind me you are," snidely remarked Randall. Willie knew he was right. He never could out run Randall.

The order came down the line. "Fix bayonets. Prepare to move forward at the double quick. March." The gray line began to move forward. The officers were in the front, swords drawn. The colors, to Willie and Randall's left, were being carried forward. Willie knew he needed to keep an eye on the colors, because that flag was their only way of communication in the midst of a battle. He looked over at the St. Andrews cross, blue on a red background, with 11 white stars in the cross. He had followed that flag so many times onto a field of battle. So far he had made it through with only mild injuries. The worst being in the far end of the cornfield at Sharpsburg, when after the enemy had infladed their flanks, when fighting hand-to-hand had ensued. Bayoneting, clubbing with the butt of the guns and pure fist-fighting early that morning had occurred. The Yankee had hit him upside the head with the gun butt, dropping him to his knees, but he had swung his own gun butt catching the Yankee on his knee and dropping him with a thud to the ground. Willie then used his bayonet to dispatch the big Yankee. That lump on the side of his head and the ball grazing his shoulder was his worst injuries. Randall had taken a Yankee ball in the thigh at Sharpsburg, one in the arm at Olustee, one had cut his ear at the second battle of Cold Harbor and twisted his ankle one-time near Richmond. Other than that, he had escaped serious injury too, although the leg wound could've been serious had the mini ball hit a measure further to the right. They were two lucky guys to have been fighting over three and a half years with no more malady than that.

As the gray line crossed the field. Yankee artillery cut loose upon them. As the shells exploded on left and right, Willie saw brave men in gray fall to the ground. They pressed forward. Then they heard the musketry cut loose from the breastworks. It sounded like a sheet tearing. More men in gray fell. The order "charge" was given and the brave southern soldiers turned double quick into a full run toward the enemy's face. They had yet to fire but as they closed the gap between them and the breastworks, they stopped just long enough to unleash a volley into the enemy. Willie saw men in blue crumble and fall to the ground as they pressed forward again. Willie looked to his left and saw Randall about three steps ahead of him, just as he had predicted earlier. They mounted the breastworks, and again hand-to-hand combat of the worst sort ensued. Willie rammed his bayonet into one blue clad soldier, removing it and swinging the butt catching another one beside the head. It was as vicious a hand-to-hand as he had encountered. It was like in Sharpsburg that morning and he turned just in time to see Joseph catch a mini ball directly in his chest and slump forward. Sherman's men had never faced the Army of Northern Virginia nor had they faced the Twenty-seventh Georgia before now, and they were going to know what other Yankees had known in Virginia and in Maryland and in Florida and in parts of North Carolina and South Carolina. This was a tough, seasoned group of men. They fought savagely and the blue bellies began to withdraw. Unfortunately, there were no reinforcements to come into their line and strengthen it, so they could push the Yankees all the way back to South Carolina. Eventually the gray line had to withdraw. Randall was limping using his musket is a crutch. So Willie grabbed him by the shoulder and helped him as they returned to their original line.

"I caught a Yankee ball in the leg Willie!" said Randall painfully. "It burns like the devil, but I don't think he got a bone, just meat. It is like a repeat of Sharpsburg.

Willie could see that Randall's pant leg was covered with blood and really began to worry about his best friend. Was he gonna' bleed to death? Was he gonna' make it? All of these questions ran through Willie's brain as he looked at Randall slumped to the ground, trying to tie a rag around his wound over his pants. Willie grabbed his pig sticker and split Randall's pant leg open, exposing the wound. It was his left thigh, and it was bleeding terribly. Reaching into his haversack, Willie produced a rag of cotton and gave it to Randall.

"Push that tight against that wound, Randall, so that maybe the bleeding will stop," said Willie remembering what the surgeons had taught him at Sharpsburg and Camp Milton as he helped care for the wounded on those occasions. Obediently Randall held the cotton rag tightly against the

wound. Sergeant Mann came along the line to assess the casualties.
Several of their boys were still over there on the breastwork, including
Joseph Crapps, and there were quite a few being tended to with wounds to,
their arms and legs, mostly. Willie looked back at Randall who was
turning a little pale. "You all right Randall?"

"It hurts a mite, but I believe I'll make it," replied Randall. He
was still pressing the cotton cloth against the wound. "I believe the
bleeding is slowing somewhat!"

Willie wished he had something to give Randall for pain, but
Randall didn't drink liquor, and Willie didn't have any anyway. As the
two armies licked their wounds, they began to prepare for what the next
day might bring.

"You reckon we gonna' fight again today?" inquired Randall.

"You ain't gonna' fight no more today, my friend." answered
Willie. "You gonna be put on the casualty list for this battle. After the
surgeon looks at you, they may send you to the hospital."

Randall quickly retorted, "I ain't gonna go to no hospital. People
die there. I ain't gonna die so there ain't no need for me to go there."
Randall's rationale was a little fuzzy, but Willie surmised he must not be
feeling too bad now. They brought a wagon along to load up the
wounded, to carry them to the surgeon's tent. After protesting somewhat,
Randall climbed up in the wagon. Willie wondered if he'd ever see his
friend again. Randall was right that lots of his friends who had gone to the
hospital did not return. Willie and Randall had friends buried all over
Maryland and Virginia and other places they had fought. He watched as
the wagon bounced along over the field taking his friend to the surgeon.
The 18th and 19th of March, 1865 were dark days in the history of the
Confederate States of America. It marked what would become the last
battle in the Eastern Theater of war. Willie had seen Private Bill Burke on
the wagon with Randall. He also heard that Lieutenant Crosby had been

captured, most likely wounded on that breastwork, but hopefully not dead. Joseph's brother John had been captured along with Willie's cousin Ben.

Lieutenant Colonel Bussey had been in command of the Regiment during this engagement. He gathered the troops together as they moved away from Bentonville. They were expecting another fight if they stayed there and the commanders did not feel that they were up to another one right away. Willie went to the surgeon's tent. He found Randall still sitting outside holding that piece of bloody cotton cloth on the wound.

"The surgeon ain't seen you yet?" Willie asked as he approached.

"He looked at it, and told me to do just what you told me to do, which was hold this piece of cloth up against it so wouldn't bleed. He said I was lucky that it didn't catch the bone or he would've had to take my leg off. It'd be hard to run in the River swamp with one leg when we get home." Randall's sense of humor was still with him.

Just then the surgeon emerged from his tent and asked Willie if he wanted to help out again like he had in Florida. Willie sensing that was a chance to help out and to keep track of Randall agreed. "Here's your first patient," he said, pointing at Randall. "Clean up that wound and get a fresh bandage on it before he catches something from the filthy rag that he's been holding there." Willie obliged, got a bucket of water with which Randall quickly washed the wound using that water and a clean rag. Willie placed a bandage on Randall's leg and said, "that'll be five cents sir!" He joked at Randall.

"You'll have to wait till I get paid 'cause, I ain't got no money on me at the time. I spent my last nickel in Kinston the other day. I bought a potato with it. Ate that sucker raw too! Could have eat the vine if I had it," quipped Randall. "You know we ain't been paid since before Fort Fisher, remember."

"It's been longer than that since we had mail," remarked Willie. Suddenly he noticed a familiar form approaching on his left. "Father? Is that you?"

"Yes, son. I sure am glad to see you alive. I wasn't sure if you had survived to this day, and I still could whup you for running off in '61 and breaking your Mama's heart," said his father, as Willie sprung to his feet and grabbed his father in an embrace.

"I'm so glad to see you're alive too, father. Where were you in the fight?" Willie inquired

"Our Regiment merged with the First Georgia Sharpshooters after the battle of Franklin, due to the fact that those of us who followed General Cleburne into the center of the battle that day were chewed up pretty bad up near the Carter house. The Carter's son was killed in their backyard on that day of fightin' Yankees. We lost quite a few men, several from home on that day."

"Hello, Willie," a voice came from behind sounding familiar. Willie looked around, and it was George who was his father's old friend and was in the same regiment as his father. "I heard you and Randall were in Virginia fightin' with Colquitt."

"Hello yourself, Mister George," said Willie as he grasped his hand in a firm handshake. "I haven't seen you in almost four years."

"I believe you've grown some," said George. "Randall, what's wrong with your leg?"

"Caught a Yankee ball today," answered Randall. "It burned like the devil."

"Aw shucks! You're one of them young, thick blooded whippersnappers. You'll get over it," remarked George. "William we better get back to camp, before the Sergeant misses us and turns us in as absent without leave."

William said somberly, "Son, I better go for now. I may can get permission to come back and visit now that I know where your unit is. I'll see you later, son."

"Good to see you, father," answered Willie. "and even better to see that you're alive since I haven't gotten any mail from home since we were on the Petersburg line. Have you heard from home?"

"Not since we left after the battle at Atlanta. We had been moving so fast mail couldn't catch up with us anyway. I'll be back," said his father.

As Willie watched his father and Mister George, leaving he felt more melancholy about home than he had a long time. It was sure good to see him and even better to see he was unharmed. Willie turned back to Randall to see how his patient was doing and saw him chewing on a piece of hardtack. "Where did you get that? Is there anymore?" asked Willie.

Grinning as he reached into his haversack Randall said, "I got two of these hardtacks when they came around. I didn't know if I was gonna' see you or not and would've eaten both of them too, if you had not come to see about me." Randall handed the piece of hardtack to Willie saying, "You better soak it in some water first or you are apt to break your teeth if you try to bite it without first soaking it."

Willie took his tin cup out of the haversack and poured some water in it from his canteen. He then placed the piece of hardtack in the cup and sat it down. "How long will it take a'fore I can eat it?"

"It'll take a little while. If I'd been hit by one of these instead of that Yankee ball, I probably wouldn't be here now," Randall smartly answered.

After a few minutes, Willie was able to eat the piece of hardtack. It wasn't so bad. He then began to tend to some of the other patients that the surgeon had assigned to him. His regiment had paid a terrible price in the assault that day. He looked over to the side of the surgeon's tent and saw the arms and legs piled there. He knew that several of his compatriots had lost limbs due to the action today and they would return home in a diminished capacity.

It would be hard to plow a mule with one leg. Some of them would never be able to farm again. If they did not have someone to do the plowing, they would have a hard time making a living. Willie spent the next few days helping the surgeon. When Randall was released from his care, they returned to their company. As they looked around they noticed that there were several missing and wondered about the fate of each. They stayed encamped near Greensboro until April 26, when they got word that General Johnston had met with General Sherman and had surrendered his army. They had been meeting for two days, trying to work out the terms of surrender. General Sherman had originally wanted to give them the same terms that General Grant had given to General Lee but after the assassination of President Lincoln the politicians in Washington were going to make it tougher on these Confederates.

Chapter Nine: Going Home

After taking the oath of allegiance to the United States, the Appling County boys of the Twenty-seventh, Forty-Seventh and Fifty-fourth Georgia gathered together to discuss how to make the trip back home. They did not have horses, and they understood that General Sherman's men had tied the railroad tracks up in "Sherman's bow ties" in Georgia and in South Carolina. Unless the tracks were repaired, they would be destined to try to walk home. They all set out heading south. There were actually some trains with tracks intact between them and Columbia, South Carolina, so all the men in gray piled into the cars on those trains heading south. In Columbia they had to again walk. They walked for days. These were men who, at times, had forced marched over 20 miles a day. These men were now worn down, tired and hungry, as there made their way home.

Once, as they were trying to make their way across the Savannah River, Willie noticed some squirrels in the hardwood trees on the edge of the swamp.

"I wish I had my old Springfield. I'd pop us one or two of them squirrels. I hated that I had to stack it at Greensboro," said Willie.

"I didn't stack my Colt's pistol," said Randall. "It is still here in my haversack. You think you can hit one of them furry critters with a pistol?"

"It should be just like a short rifle. Give me that thing," said Willie.

Willie took the Colt's pistol and finding a tree to lean up against, took careful aim and fired. The cat squirrel came tumbling down the tree. In a few minutes, he bagged the second one. Randall was already getting his pot which was full of water hot. He told the others to look around and see if they can come up with some kind of root, or a potato or something. Randall was getting ready to make one of his famous stews.

Willie and his daddy quickly cleaned the squirrels washing them in the creek. After cutting the squirrels up, Randall dropped them in the pot as they sat around waiting for the stew to cook. They enjoyed a sumptuous meal that night, which was a rarity on this trip. Willie slept better than he had in a long time.

It took almost a month to get to the Altamaha River. Willie, his father, Randall, George and several others from the county who had been traveling together climbed onto Stafford's Ferry and crossed the Altamaha heading for Middleton's store which was not very far from his home.

Willie's mother was feeding the hogs, all three of them, when she turned to see two men approaching the cabin. Realizing it was her husband and her son, she screamed, "Lizzy! Come here quick! Your father and Willie are home!" She ran as fast as she could to greet them. First hugging and kissing her husband and then grabbing and squeezing her son in her arms. "I was afraid I would never see either of you again! It was my nightmare every night that both of you would be buried in some foreign soil and I would never know where you were. It is great to see you."

Suddenly this attractive, grown girl came running from the cabin. "Lizzy! Is that you, girl?" her father said as he grabbed her up, lifting her from the ground and clutching her tightly to his chest. "You are a sight for sore eyes!"

"Yes Pa! It's me. You two look good although you are both thin, dirty and tired looking," she remarked, looking them over from their feet to the top of their heads. "I bet you could stand some cornbread and a little bacon. Grandma taught me how to make cornbread like she does. Ain't that right ma?" She was beside herself, as she also had wondered if she would ever see either of them again, and now they both had walked right up into the yard. "We heard the war was over when we went to the store to get some salt. After you're washed and fed, you'll have to tell us about all your adventures both of you." She grabbed her brother and hugged him tight. They had always been close.

"We need to talk about your new boyfriend, sis. Do I know him?" said Willie, like an overprotective brother.

"You do. It's Michael Watkins." She blushed as she made the statement.

"Has he grown up?" asked Willie. "He can't be that old!"

"Yes. He was almost old enough to join Captain Ben Milikin's militia company toward the end of the war. He tried to and Captain Ben sent him home."

103

"Benjamin Milikin is still alive? The last time I saw the sergeant he was leaning up beside a tree at the end of the cornfield near Sharpsburg. He had been hit in the leg and was dragged there before we withdrew, by Blue Sapp," Willie said with wonder in his voice.

"He was a Yankee prisoner for a while, and then was paroled. He was placed in the invalid corps, because he does not walk well, but when he heard that General Sherman was coming through Georgia he gathered up a company of young boys and old men to go fight him. They elected him captain," said Willie's mother.

"Well I'll be dad burned," exclaimed Willie.

They visited for a little and then moved toward the cabin. This was the first time since the summer of 1861 that the whole family had been together.

"I'm supposed to meet Randall down at the whirl hole for a swim in a little while. That'll be the best bath I've had in a long time. I may just soak in there for an hour or two, but I would rather eat first if that's okay with you two," said Willie in a voice much deeper than his mother had remembered. Her son had grown up to become a man in this last, almost 4 years.

After sitting down to a meal which included Lizzy's cornbread, that did taste like grandma's, Willie leaned back in that straight backed chair from the table and said, "That is the best food I have had in almost 4 years. I cannot tell you how good it is to be home with you all."

"Willie, looking around it appears we have plenty of work to do. I know your mother has done all she could do, and Lizzy too. But the place really needs some attention, and I know two men who can give it to it," said his father, who upon looking at him appeared proud of him.

"We can start on it first thing in the morning, and it will pleasure me to work alongside you again. If it is all right with you all, I'll go down to the creek and see if Randall is at the whirl hole yet! I feel nasty," said Willie, as he rose from the chair and headed toward the door grabbing his jacket." I might as well wash this while I'm down there."

"No. You give that to me, son," said his mother. "I haven't washed either of your things in so long, I've got to see if I still know how to do it." She took his jacket from him and said, "You can wash your pants and drawers though, while you're down there. I wouldn't want you prancin' around naked, although since the nearest neighbors are two miles away, no one probably would see you 'cept me and Lizzie, and we don't want to."

Willie took the shortcut through the woods, and as he approached the creek, he heard splashing He cautiously approached not knowing who was making the splashing noise. He peered from behind a tree, and there was Randall, skinny dipping in the creek like the old days. He quickly shucked off his clothes and brogans and hit the water with the giant splash. They must have swum for an hour more, before they got out and slipped their wet clothes on. They had washed them while they were in the creek and hung them on a limb. They had not dried. They sat on a log there by the creek that was still there after four years. They talked about the war. They talked about their travels. They talked about all that they had seen and done. Then they finally got to the subject of the two girls at Teabeauville. They wondered if they were still there. They wondered if they had gotten married. They wondered if they even remembered them. They made the decision that they would write letters to the girls and take them up to Middleton's store, which was a local post office and inquire of them.

After about two weeks, Willie and his father had the farm in good shape. The crops that they planted might be late but if the weather held up, it would give them an abundance of food stores for the winter. One of the sows had pigs, and they were hopeful to grow enough food to fatten them out, so that by the time the cold weather came, they could have a hog killing and smoke some meat for the next year. Gray, the old horse, had done a fine job pulling that plow, and although she was older than Willie, she was still a worker. They had seen some of their friends who had made it back. Some of them were missing arms and legs but they were still alive.

It was July 4, and Willie and Randall had gone to the store to see if their families had enough credit with Mrs. Middleton to get a few supplies that were needed at home. When she saw them, Mrs. Middleton said, "You boys both have some mail." Their hearts leapt, and they couldn't wait to get the letters and open them. They went outside the store, and sat on the old bench that was made from a split log and read their letters. Yes, the girls had remembered them. No, they were not married. And they both thought it would be great to see them again. The boys didn't walk back home but hopped and skipped and jumped all the way there.

Lizzie was curious about how her brother Willie was acting. She had never seen him act like that before. She inquired as to the contents of the letter, but Willie wasn't about to tell her what was in there. His mind drifted to Sally's blue eyes and pretty smile. He thought of her long blonde hair and her sweet sounding voice. He could not wait until they could take a trip to Doctortown and get on that train bound for Teabeauville.

SALLY

MARY

Chapter Ten: Courtin'

Although Willie and Randall had helped their families planting crops, none had matured and been harvested. There was no money to be had in the family. Willie learned that folks would get by the train track and hop on an empty car and ride. The conductors, knowing that no one had any money, would leave them alone and allow that to happen. In two weeks, Willie and Randall met on the road to Doctortown. They walked there and waited for a train. Asking around, they found that one was due in about three hours so they hung around, waiting for the train. They heard stories how when the Yankees came to tear the trestle down, so that the Confederate's could not reinforce behind Sherman as he went into Savannah, that a company of dismounted cavalry of Clinch's Fourth Georgia and a bunch of old men and young boys had put a whipping on them, sending them back to Walthourville to tear the track up there to prevent the reinforcing.

Sure enough in about four hours, the train pulled in. Willie and Randall walked up and down the train, until they found a car that was empty and the door was open. They scampered in and sat there waiting. Eventually they felt the jolt as the locomotive started west. Since they didn't know how long the ride would be or just how to know if they were in Teabeauville one of them had to be a look-out the entire time. They paid attention as the train passed through stops located every ten miles. They later learned that the stops were spaced out so that the locomotives would be able to take on wood and water sufficient enough to make their trips. Tthey now had been told that the stops were 10 miles apart. They passed through Reddishville, Screven, Patterson, Blackshear and finally arrived at Teabeauville. They jumped out of the car, brushing the dust off their clothes and started walking toward the white house that Sally had indicated she lived in. Their hearts were in their throats as they first approached the door, and Willie knocked on it. An older lady that resembled Sally came to the door. Willie almost died. What would he say? Was this a mistake?

"May I help you, young man?" she inquired.

Willie could hardly speak. He had never shown fear in battle as he faced the enemy, but he was scared to death right now. "Is Sally home, ma'am?"

"Yes, and whom shall I say is calling?" she replied

"Er! Er! Tell her it is Willie. The soldier she met here over a year ago. The.... The.... The one who wrote her the letter," stammered Willie almost unable to contain himself

"Son, just sit over there on the bench, on the porch, and I will see if she is able to come and greet you," she said sensing Willie's nervousness and trying to set him at ease.

Willie and Randall sat there on that bench for what seemed to be an eternity, when suddenly the most beautiful girl Willie had ever seen emerged from the front door of the house. "Willie! Randall! It is so good to see you again. I knew you said you were coming, but I didn't know when so I didn't have time to fix up any." Willie knew that if she was not fixed up now he might not be able to stand to look at her when she was.

"Mother, the boys and I are going to go to see Mary if it's all right with you," she called back into the house.

"I have no objection to you accompanying these two fine young gentlemen to Mary's house," said her mother, much to Willie's relief.

They walked two houses over and Willie and Randall sat on the steps as Sally went to the door. Sally went inside, and in short order, returned with Mary tagging along behind. "I see you two boys made it through the war in one piece," said Mary. "I'm sure glad to see that you did."

Randall was so bashful he could hardly say a word. This valiant warrior who would crash into the enemy's front like a wild man was taken aback by the pretty brunette in his front. No Yankee had ever scared him that much. The two couples walked all around Teabeauville, which was not very large. Had it not been for the railroad, it most likely wouldn't even be there at all. There were lots of ex-soldiers in uniform around town. Willie was glad that he and Randall had some clothes that didn't look like they were still in the Army. After being shown all the way around town by the two girls, they returned to Sally's front porch, where they sat for hours talking. Randall finally got comfortable enough to open up and tell them some of his adventures as a soldier. Mary could not believe that he had been wounded in the arm and in the leg twice and was still alive. Sally could not believe that Willie had made it all the way through with just getting hit upside the head at Sharpsburg.

They really got to know each other well and it was with regrets when the boys heard the train whistle and saw the eastbound train approaching. It was then they knew they were going to have to leave and go home. With a promise to write, and the boys promised that they would make the train ride again to see them, they parted. All the way home on the train all they could talk about was those girls. They finally realized that they most likely were in love and did not know what in the world to do about it. They had no land and they had no jobs. They had no money. They had nothing to offer those girls, but they determined that one day that they would do everything they could to put themselves in position to ask Sally and Mary for their hands in marriage, one day in the future.

After returning home, they worked hard on the farms. They picked up extra jobs and tried to save every penny they could get their hands on. They even operated Stafford's Ferry, earning a commission on the tolls they took in. They made several more trips to Teabeauville to see the girls, and eventually by the next spring Willie had bought a little 40 acre piece of land. Randall had helped him clear that land, so that he would be able to plant a crop on a few acres there. A month later, Randall bought 35 acres near Willie's land. They cleared that up and got it ready for Randall to plant. They had to borrow their families' horses and plows to cultivate the land. By the next summer they had saved up some money and decided they needed to build a cabin on each piece of land. All the neighbors around scheduled two log rollings, one for each house. It amazed Willie and Randall that all those neighbors could get together, chop down the trees, notch them and stack them to the point of putting a roof on in one day. The womenfolk from around the community came that morning. They cooked some beef and venison to feed the workers and had a whole hog, buried in a pit full of coals, that cooked all day long to feed them at days end. It was great to live in a community of friends that would help each other out in time of need.

For the next few weeks, the boys spent every spare minute trying to get a roof on the cabins and chinking the cracks between the logs. Finally, both cabins were completed. The boys then wrote letters to Sally and Mary, saying that they would soon arrive at Teabeauville to visit with them. The date was set for the visit so that the girls would be expecting them. At the appointed time the two boys made the trip to Teabeauville via the Gulf and Atlantic railroad line from Doctortown. Willie had grown a mustache but Randall remained clean-shaven.

When they arrived at Teabeauville the girls were waiting at the train station pretty as ever. As they visited, they were able to meet with the girls' fathers and asked for their hands in marriage. Both fathers were coy for a bit. They inquired as to how they planned to support their daughters, which gave the boys the opening to speak of their little farms that they had started. Seemingly pleased with the boy's answers, both fathers agreed. They went back outside, where both girls were waiting, and told them that their fathers had agreed to the marriages. All four were beside themselves. They set a date. The place would be the little Methodist Church there at Teabeauville. Mary was so excited that she grabbed Randall and kissed him square on the mouth. He almost dropped in his tracks. Sally was excited, but not so carried away as to have a public display of affection right there in Teabeauville. Not in front of God and everybody.

The boys returned home and began to make preparations. When the day came, both of the families went to Doctortown and boarded the train in the passenger car. They took the trip to Teabeauville together. Willie and Randall had never ridden in a passenger car. They were used to being in a box car, so this was another special thing for them. Their mothers were so excited at the prospect of having daughters-in-law that they talked to each other all the way there.

The train arrived at Teabeauville. There was Sally and her family, Mary and her family and what appeared to be the preacher. The families took rooms in the boardinghouse by the track, and the boys with their future brides spent the afternoon together, walking around and discussing their future. On the next day the most beautiful double wedding that Teabeauville had ever seen occurred in that little Methodist Church. The whole town turned out for it. The church was full. That afternoon the two families with the new additions boarded the train for Doctortown. The girls both kissed and hugged their family. They waved goodbye to all of their friends, and promised that it was not too far to Appling County that they could not come back and visit sometime.

When they arrived, the girls were delighted with their new homes and quickly began to make them their own. The two best of friends, who had married two more best of friends were neighbors and would see lots of each other. Willie and Randall went in business together cutting timber and rafting it down the Altamaha to Doctortown to the new sawmill that was opened there. They continued to cut timber and purchase additional land with the profits until both men had holdings of over a thousand acres.

They continued to clear the land and plant crops and became quite comfortable. They began to read the law. Randall's reading had improved tremendously as he worked hard at it.

One Sunday afternoon, Willie saddled his black gelding and decided to ride down near the creek. He was reminiscing about the days of his youth and all things he and Randall used to get into. As he approached the "Whirl Hole", he heard splashing. Drawing nearer, he spotted Randall's gray stallion tied to a tree limb and eating the tender grasses at the base of the tree. He looked to see Randall's clothes on a limb. Randall was splashing around like a wood duck in a beaver pond. Hearing the hoof beats he turned around and shouted.

"Hey, Willie! Shuck off your clothes and come join me. The water is fine and cool today," chatted Randall.

"Might as well. I don't have anything better to do," remarked Willy, as he swung off his horse and started preparing for another "skinny dip" like they had done so many times before. Lots of things in their life had changed, but they still remained the same two boys, just a little older.

No one in that community in 1861 would have ever imagined that Willie would later become a State Senator and that Randall would become a judge. The life experiences of both boys had aided their education. Afterward they were to continue raising their families and continue on with the rest of their lives along the Altamaha River.

Like many Confederate soldiers, they came back to their homes and communities. They led their communities through reconstruction and on into the 20th century. They were the backbones of the growth of small towns and counties all over the South. Without their efforts, their communities would not have grown, would not have prospered and would not have become what they are today. To them we, who now live in those communities, owe an eternal debt of gratitude for both their sacrifice in the war and their sacrifice in building their communities.

I'm going,

Then I'm going too.

Home

About the Author

William A. Bowers, Jr. was born August 5, 1947 in St. Augustine, Florida to William Alfred Bowers Sr. and Lora Elizabeth Tuten. When he was young, his family returned to Baxley, Appling County, Georgia, where he lived, was raised and educated. He is a 1965 graduate of Appling County High School, an Eagle Scout and is retired from the Georgia Department of Transportation as an Area Engineer in South Georgia. He is married to Anna Deloris Willis of Toombs County. He is a member of the First United Methodist Church in Baxley, Georgia.

For the last 22 years he has been involved in researching Confederate Units, battles and genealogy. Bill has been to almost all the places that the 27th Georgia fought and has stood where they stood in his research of this unit. He has given speeches across South Georgia concerning those Confederate units and their part in the War for Southern Independence. He resides still in Appling County and has served as a scout leader for 30 years, an officer in the Appling Grays Camp #918 Sons of Confederate Veterans, the Appling County Board of Education, the First United Methodist Church Administrative Board and the Appling County Heritage Center Board of Directors.

He has published three regimental histories with *the History of the 47th Georgia Volunteer Infantry* being published in May 2013 and *the History of the 27th Georgia Volunteer Infantry* being published in February 2014. In 2016 he published *the History of the 54th Georgia Volunteer Infantry*. This completes the trilogy of Confederate Regimental Histories which encompasses the four companies of Confederate Infantry which originated in Appling County, Georgia. In 2017 he published the *Bowers Genealogy, the Descendants of Benjamin Bowers, Sr., of Pitt County, North Carolina.*

This Book, *Two Rebels from the Altamaha* is his first novel and is about two young men from Appling County, Georgia who enlisted to fight for the Confederate States of America.